RAPE *of an* ANGEL

"and all of Heaven wept"

MICHAEL SPINCOLA

Copyright © 2023 Michael Spincola.

All rights reserved. No part of this book may be reproduced, stored, or transmitted by any means—whether auditory, graphic, mechanical, or electronic—without written permission of both publisher and author, except in the case of brief excerpts used in critical articles and reviews. Unauthorized reproduction of any part of this work is illegal and is punishable by law.

ISBN: 979-8-89031-231-0 (sc)
ISBN: 979-8-89031-232-7 (hc)
ISBN: 979-8-89031-233-4 (e)

Because of the dynamic nature of the Internet, any web addresses or links contained in this book may have changed since publication and may no longer be valid. The views expressed in this work are solely those of the author and do not necessarily reflect the views of the publisher, and the publisher hereby disclaims any responsibility for them.

One Galleria Blvd., Suite 1900, Metairie, LA 70001
1-888-421-2397

THE BOOK TEAM

Editor: Francine Zaggia

Research & Development: Rev. Mariano Gargiulo

Illustrator, Front Cover "The Angel": Jon Paul Ferrara

Graphic Designer, Back Cover "The Scapula": Paul Kopel

CONTENTS

For Steven 1
Reverend Mother Elizabeth Pia 4
A Mission on the Serengeti 7
The Tanzania Mission Team 11
Welcome! 16
Ten Years After 21
The African Outrage 27
Dad's Office 33
Ground Zero 37
The Upper West Side 42
The Crazed Man 44
Sergeant Gina 50
Baby-Sister 58
Blessed-Sisters in Training 62
The Ordeal 81
The Hospital 94
Out of Nowhere 97
Sister Antonia 104
The Devil 108
The Archangel 115
Back in Heaven 122
Kitty in the Basement 125

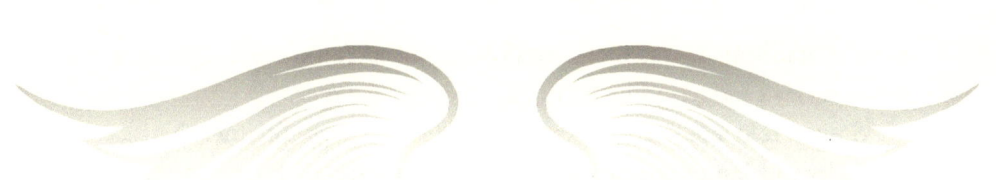

FOR STEVEN

While writing this book, my mom called me at a friend's home and asked me to, "Come home right away." So I immediately raced home to Cliffside Park with only a million scenarios of what I would find – all with bad outcomes. When I arrived home I found my mom Maureen, my brother Frank and Uncle Eddie – all with grim looks on their faces. My mother apologized for needing to tell me such sad news in this fashion but felt it was something that needed to be said in person. "We have terrible news, Michael. We lost *our* Steven today."

Steven Spincola was my brother with the truly angelic face and impish persona, a very dangerous combination of traits. He was the second of four sons of Frank and Maureen Spincola. He was only 10 days shy of his 55th birthday when he passed away. He was our family's bright light.

Steven was real cool. A party only needed beer, food, music and Steven for something crazy to happen. In fairness, he was also banned from many restaurants and gin mills throughout northeastern Bergen County for being overtly rambunctious. Don't misunderstand, Steven loved his family and worked hard. He was one of the best paperhangers around. He could, like his father, name just about every seated senator and congressman in America.

On holidays and special occasions he would energize a party with songs, acrobatic stunts, jokes and dances; he could even growl like Roy Orbison. Every guy wanted to hang with him and all the ladies wanted him as their *dream date*. A list of his antics could fill several volumes. Here is just one example of his spontaneous creativity:

One afternoon, Steven called me at work saying he and his *comparé* Pete Zilocchi had an extra ticket for tonight's World Series Game 1 at

Yankee Stadium. It was October 1981, and the Yankees were playing the Los Angeles Dodgers. The extra ticket wasn't for me.

Steven told me that Yankee owner, George Steinbrenner, had asked movie legend James Cagney to throw out the first pitch hoping the NYC born actor would be a good luck charm for the Yanks. However, MLB Commissioner, Bowie Kuhn, told the Yankees that the actor would *not* be allowed to participate in the game's festivities because Cagney "*glorified gangsterism*" during his movie career. Cagney just happened to be Steven's favorite actor. So he said, "I need a bedsheet sign to hang from the Yankee Stadium rafters." Oh boy, someone just poked the bear.

He wanted me to call our artist friend Carlo Basile and, in return for his efforts, he could go to the game with them. Carlo was excited and quickly agreed. He asked what Steven wanted painted on the sign. I told him that Steven needed:

PUBLIC ENEMY KUHN!
WHERE'S OUR YANKEE DOODLE CAGNEY?

That Tuesday evening the World Series was on ABC-TV (Channel 7 in New York) with Howard Cosell flying solo in the pregame booth. Cosell explained the Cagney predicament giving an incredulous type critique of the commissioner's decision. Then they showed the sign hanging in the upper right field stands on television!

That alone was not as easy as one might think. The Bronx's evening breezes forced the guys to reinforce the hanging bed sheet with duct tape while stepping over the guardrail and dangerously leaning over a 30' drop to the lower deck. Hanging a sign was not really allowed at Yankee Stadium because so many people had made signs throughout the season depicting George Steinbrenner in a Nazi Storm Trooper's uniform. His outfit was always complete with black jackboots, a riding crop and a Picklehaube, the spiked German helmet. But there was Steven's creation hanging majestically hanging in Yankee Stadium with a spot on commentary regarding the situation.

ABC-TV showed Cagney sitting in Steinbrenner's private box pointing out toward the sign, nodding his head in agreement. Channel 7 showed the sign again – this time for about 30 seconds. And finally, Howard Cosell says, in his own unique vernacular: ***"AND - THAT - SIGN - SAYS - IT - ALL!"*** (Sign hanging Yankee fans just followed the lead of Cartoonist Bill Gallo. Mr. Gallo, of the New York Daily News, had created a caricature of George Steinbrenner based on the boss's dictator-like ways called: General von Steingrabber.)

A security guard did yell at them to take the sign down. But after he received a message on his walkie-talkie he said, "OK, leave it up, but don't step over the railing." Someone decided the sign deserved to be there.

The very next evening at Game 2, a very embarrassed Bowie Kuhn had a change of heart and allowed Cagney to throw out the first pitch. Again Pete and Steven were there and it was electric.

That was Steven. God bless him. See ya soon. You won't be hard to find. We'll go into the part of Limbo having the most fun.

P.S. Your beautiful daughter Leigh married Bryan and is very happy.

Your son Stevie has grown to become a wonderful and successful young man.

Your brother,
Michael

* * * *

As I've been known to say, I write what I feel. I do my best but I'll never rise to the story telling levels of Bobby Oppermann, Charlie Gobel, Vince Gargiulo or Frank Frato.

Mike Spin

REVEREND MOTHER ELIZABETH PIA

Born in 1940, Elizabeth Pia grew up just outside of Paris, France. As a child she survived World War II and as a teen she felt her Parisian world was baroque and colorful. She was greatly influenced by the now popular American music and culture but she found serenity in the spirituality of Rome and the Holy See.

In 1958 she entered the Sorbonne and would graduate with majors in both religious studies and Anatomy & Physiology. Early in her senior year she had joined an on-campus part of Mother Teresa's The Order of Missionaries of Charity and received their permission to continue her studies, earning duel Masters Degrees in 1966.

In the fall of 1966 she was assigned to a Paris hospital emergency room that was sponsored by the Missionaries of Charity Novitiate. Pia knew she was doing important work but a part of her always felt like something in her life was missing. During her next four years working in the ER, Pia had been formulating a plan for a Mission of her own. It started unintentionally when she overheard two Jesuit priests discussing their upcoming trip to Africa and the continent's overwhelming thirst to learn about Jesus. From there, it began to take on a life of its own with every minute she spent in the ER. Finally, Pia had found her direction and could keep quiet about it no longer. She needed to write her Mother Superior as she desperately needed her counsel.

* * * *

Just like Mother Teresa twenty years before, Pia's project would take more than a decade to develop before it came to fruition. The first step would be to petition the Holy See for its support. In the spring of 1970, Pia met with the Congregation for the Evangelation of People. One must appeal to the Vatican council for project approval and financial support. Pia presented a detailed outline of her missionary plans and the council agreed that they would pass it along for approval. Six months later, the report and recommendation was sent to the Institute for the Works of Religion (IOR) of the Vatican Bank. Six more months went by when Pia was finally called to the Vatican to receive their official approval.

As Pia was nervously walking into the council chambers, a little woman touched her on the sleeve. It was Mother Teresa. Pia was stunned, realizing Teresa was there to wield her magic for her if needed. "Mother, hello!" She didn't know what else to say. Mother Teresa just smiled and hugged her very valued student. She whispered in French, "Toujours garder Dieu dans votre coeur, ma fille." (Always keep God in your heart, my daughter.) Pia's mission project received full support from the Vatican.

With her newly approved funds and plans in tow, Pia commissioned the full renovation of an old, abandoned novitiate she bought just outside of Paris. The work took all of 1971 but was transformed into a strong and solid home base that she could launch and oversee her very ambitious undertaking. Pia named the structure The Blessed-Sisters' Novitiate which would house the Blessed-Sisters' Formation Program. Her project would officially begin in September of 1972 when Pia was formally installed as its Reverend Mother.

Ten carefully selected aspirants would become the Novitiate's first class. Among them was prize recruit Gina Rose Formaggio from Convent Station, New Jersey. Her project would take Mother Teresa's rescue work one step further by teaching stability through formal and practical education. Pia was absolutely thrilled that her idea was about to become a reality.

Mother Pia's most incredible moment occurred almost a decade later. Pia walked into her office to find a beautiful child sitting in her chair. The child smiled and said, "I'm Kitty and I'm six years old." Pia was amused at her precociousness. "How did you get here little one?" Kitty answered, "Michael brought me but you can ask him yourself. He's standing right behind you." Pia turned around to see an incredibly beautiful celestial being quietly standing in the corner. "God has been watching your work Mother and ordered me to bring this young lady to help you."

Her mind reeling at the thought, Pia asked, "Are you the *Archangel* Michael?" "Yes, good mother, I am he." In that awful moment when your brain has not caught up to your tongue, a wide-eyed Pia looked up at him and asked, "Are you sure?" Seeing this divine being looking at her with an expression that said, "Really?" Pia quickly gathered her thoughts and said, "Please thank our Lord for His divine assistance; I'm very grateful." "You're very welcome Mother. I will return to Heaven with your message as I now must take my leave. Kitty, as you've already been told, Mother Pia is your guardian here on Earth. Help her, child." The Archangel then dissipated into light and mist as did Pia's memory of the extraordinary events that occurred that day. For now she would only be able to remember that an orphaned child had been left in her care. Looking closely at her new ward, Pia couldn't help but wonder: Who would really be taking care of whom?

A MISSION ON THE SERENGETI

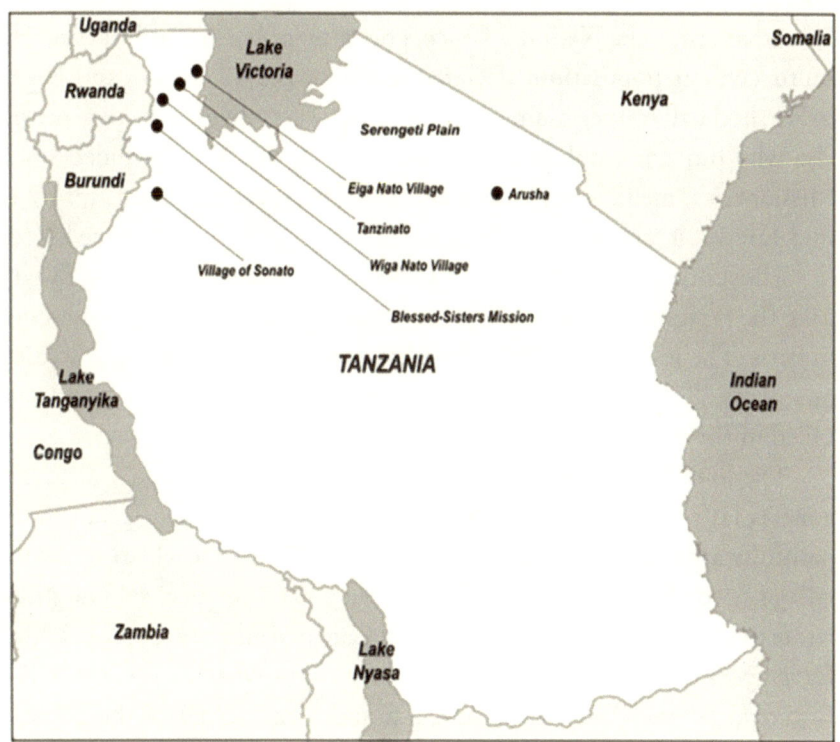

Tanzania, a country about the same size as Egypt, is located in east Africa. Within its borders you will find the small town of Tanzinato with about 5,000 inhabitants. Tanzinato sits in the northwestern part of Tanzania, about 10 miles east of Lake Victoria and is flanked by tribal villages, the largest being Wiga Nato. The town used to receive up to a half a million visitors each year, mostly film makers and missionaries doing evangelical work. The rest were vacationers who wanted to see African animals in the wild. However, the close proximity of Rwanda to this particular section of Tanzania put an abrupt halt to any kind of tourism in the area.

The turbulent political climate between the Hutu-led government and the Rwandan Patriotic Front led to The Rwandan Civil War in 1990. Three years later, a cease-fire agreement was reached with definitive plans to enact the Arusha Accords which had been signed in Arusha, Tanzania. Yet evil was not finished with Rwanda. In 1994, members of the core political elite known as the akazu whose members were much of the Rwandan army, the National Police, government-backed militias and the Hutu civilian population, declared genocide on all Tutsi's and began to methodically rape, maim and kill their Tutsi neighbors and anyone else who did not emphatically support the akazu. This included Jesuit Missionaries, medical volunteers and UN Peacekeepers. From April 7 to mid-July 1994, an estimated 500,000–1,000,000 Rwandans were killed.

The Jesuit missionary priests had been in Africa for hundreds of years. Like the Knights Templar 400 years before them, they too were founded in Paris. The Jesuits are priest/evangelists while the Templars were soldier/guardians. Both groups were powerful; each picked up the sword and killed in the name of God.

The lone Jesuit missionary remaining at the Wiga Nato village had gone as far as he could. The village families craved knowledge and were painfully aware of what was happening in Rwanda. The elders knew the village needed to update its culture if they were to survive. The priest wrote to the leader of his order in Rome, Cardinal Alfonso Campo, asking for help. The Cardinal, in turn, knew exactly what to do. He called Reverend Mother Elizabeth Pia, the founder and leader of the Blessed-Sisters' Formation Program in Paris, and had a lengthy and enthusiastic discussion with her about an assignment in Africa for her Blessed-Sisters. Excited about the prospect of being able to realize her dream of starting her own Mission School, Pia promised Cardinal Campo she would have an answer for him by week's end. First, she needed the advice and blessing of her Mother Superior.

Answering on the first ring, it seemed like Mother Teresa was waiting by the phone for Pia's call. She told Teresa that she was sure that the Cardinal's situation seemed like the perfect starting point to launch her project; she felt it was a Divine calling. Teresa was quick to answer, "My daughter, don't keep God waiting. If you need help, let me know." Over the years, Pia would often think about that call and wonder if what she thought was a Divine calling was merely a saintly person's intercession.

When word came back from the Cardinal confirming the construction of a new mission, the Jesuit dropped to his knees and thanked God for answering his prayers. Feeling the Earth tremble slightly beneath him, he dismissed it as a herd of animals passing by on their way to the watering hole. Had he listened more closely, he would have recognized it as mocking laughter spewing up from the depths of darkness.

* * * *

A presentation was given to the tribes by Cardinal Campo and Reverend Mother. The meeting resulted in an incredible response from the villagers. The new mission school was to be built 2 miles south of the Wiga Nato village with three Blessed-Sisters and their Reverend Mother living on campus. The Wiga Nato Village would be the first to enroll and the Sonato and Eiga Nato villages would enroll soon after. When the meeting ended, the villagers applauded, serenaded and praised them for their sacrifice and generosity. It was agreed the children would continue their education under the tutelage of the Jesuit missionary until the new Mission School was completed.

Three months after the meeting, newly appointed Reverend Mother Kitty McGuire arrived in the African jungle on August 1, 1994. She came straight from the Paris Novitiate of Blessed-Sisters and was anxious to get Pia's 'Mission Project' started. The engineers that the Paris Motherhouse had hired were asked to design a one story structure large enough to house four nuns and have four large classroom areas.

The immediate area had already been cleared of trees and brush. Moving with uncharacteristic speed, construction was nearly complete. A clear sign of the times, the area was surrounded by a twelve foot electric chain-link fence with two additional feet of looped razor wire on top.

There was also 20' of cleared space beyond the fence to keep wild animals at a safe distance from the building and its occupants.

About an inch underground and two feet out from the fence was thick gauge wire mesh to ward off things that crawl or walk low to the ground. There was also a gauzy cloth screen that draped over all the compound openings to keep out the lower flying mosquitos, flies and bees. Light gauge wire netting separately rose above the fence which sent out sonic pulses to confuse the bats, vultures, hawks and other birds of prey. Such is the way of life in the African jungle.

There was a raised metal trailer the size of two railroad cars that was hermetically sealed and refrigerated for food storage. Water and canned goods were kept on the upwind side of the building. The bathrooms were modern and used a chemical treatment system. They were located on the south side of the complex.

The main building contained a large communal room complete with kitchen, dining area and living room. The nun's personal quarters consisted of four sparse 8' x 10' bedrooms, each furnished with a wooden framed bed, a small chair and chest of drawers. The entire compound was powered by two commercial generators that ran on diesel fuel. The fuel was stored in subterranean tanks in the back of the building and was drawn by hand pump. There was enough food and fuel to last about three months. After that, all supplies would need to be replenished. Two American-made 4 x 4 capped pick-up trucks were parked in the back, near the fuel tanks.

Not by accident, the Mission's dimensions were the same ones that God had commanded Noah to use in building the Ark. [Genesis: Chapter 6, Verse 14: And the Lord said, "Make a boat from resinous wood, sealing it with tar; and construct decks and stalls throughout the ship. Make it 300 cubits by 50 cubits by 30 cubits. …And Noah did everything as God commanded him.]

An ark is anything that can take a person or a group from confusion and chaos to safety and salvation. An ark can be something physical, cognitive, emotional or spiritual; or any combination of the four. The Ark of the Covenant holds God's promise of salvation. Noah's Ark carried living creatures of every kind to safety. And the greatest ark of all is the Body of Christ. Resurrection Day, now celebrated as Easter Sunday, is what the Ark of the Christ gave us: Eternal forgiveness.

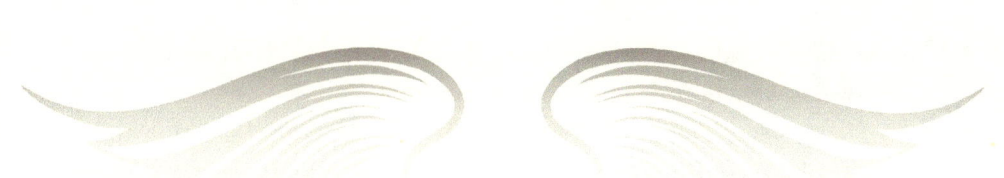

THE TANZANIA MISSION TEAM

The three Blessed-Sisters who had been carefully chosen to work with Sister Kitty at the Wiga Nato Mission met in the town of Tanzinato, on September 1, 1994. They were all well aware that they were part of a large undertaking. They would be Kitty's understudies, gleaning what they could from this very special nun. The Blessed-Sisters fearlessly came to Tanzania as women of God on the lookout for better, more efficient ways to communicate information to children and to those who desired to learn. The Sisters also knew that while Kitty was listed as being 18 years old, she had to have been in existence for much, much longer. It was truly an honor for them to be part of this elite project which was being led by an extraordinary person. Unbeknownst to them, all of Heaven was watching.

* * * *

Sister Gemma, like Kitty, was an orphan and was raised by a series of foster parents. At the age of 12, she was, quite literally, left standing on the doorstep of the Paris Novitiate. After a long search failed to reveal any information about her parents, she settled into the convent way of life. Pia was the foster mother and legal guardian of both girls until Kitty left for the States. Gemma just missed meeting Kitty, who had left only six weeks before to live for a year at the New York City Novitiate and then for 10 years with her adoptive parents in New Jersey. The tales of Kitty were never ending and her exploits would have a profound effect on Gemma. The stories were both magical and inspiring.

Eleven years later at the Paris Novitiate, a 23 year old Gemma and a 17 year old Kitty finally met. The older nuns, led by Reverend Mother Pia, delighted in singing the praises of raising Gemma and lamenting the *woebegone* days that Kitty spent with them. Kitty played along by hanging her head in mock shame to the great amusement of the older nuns. At one point Kitty shouted out, "Was I really that bad!?" Pia instantly jumped to her feet – clutched her chest and said "Mannaggia la miseria" which is Italian for "Damn misery." They all burst out laughing and came together in the middle of the room where the older nuns hugged their two grown daughters. Kitty picked that moment to publicly ask Gemma to accompany her on the African Mission in Tanzania as a teacher. Rendered speechless at the unexpected invitation for such an elite post, Gemma could only nod her consent. It's amazing how loud nuns can be when celebrating the achievements of two of their own.

* * * *

Miriam "Mira" Chevez was born in Campinas, São Paulo. The 26 year old Brazilian could still vividly recall a town official pulling up in front of her school to deliver the earth shattering news. In an instant, she had lost both her parents, the two most important people in her life. They had been involved in a fatal car crash just a few miles from their home. Only 10 years old and having no other family, Mira was sent to live in a convent in Holambra.

Reverend Mother Florence Marta and the seven nuns who lived at the Convento de Brasil saw to it that Mira was an integral part of their little family. They all loved her as if she was one of their own but it was Marta who became the most influential person in Mira's life. The love, support and wisdom she bestowed upon Mira helped to make her a first rate student in grammar school and throughout high school. When Mira expressed a strong desire to follow in Reverend Mother's footsteps serving God, Marta happily submitted Mira's application for admission into the Blessed-Sisters' Program in Paris where she was accepted.

By the time she finished the Blessed-Sisters' Program and the Sorbonne, the young woman's knowledge and style of teaching and nursing had become famous. She was becoming one of the most revered Blessed-Sisters the program had ever produced. Mira was on assignment in Columbia when she received Marta's call saying, "Sister Kitty has chosen you to be on her Tanzanian Mission Team." Shocked at the news, Mira couldn't get the words out about her new assignment or the fact that she would be working with Kitty. Marta whispered, "Child, you will need to show all your talents and skills in Africa, and you need to thank Our Lord for making your dreams come true." Mira could only say, "Mother, thank you for preparing me for this wonderful opportunity. I love you so much." After Sister hung up the phone she immediately got down on her knees and offered up prayers of thanks. She was truly blessed.

* * * *

When an Irish family has one of their own set out to serve the Lord it's something very special. In the Celtic culture, those who choose to dedicate their lives to the Lord are treated with the utmost respect and reverence.

Christina (Tina) Mary O'Dwyer was the third eldest of eight children of the O'Dwyer clan from Dublin. She worked hard to save money and also applied for financial aid to fulfill her dream of attending Trinity College in Rome. Tina wanted to study there because of all the opportunities the city offered. Dublin's Archbishop helped in both areas by sponsoring Tina's work during the summer and getting her access to many restricted places throughout Rome.

Over the years, Mother Pia had heard about a young lass from Éire who was causing the entire religious community to take notice. Pia told Kitty about this special nun and Sister thought Tina could very well be the final piece for her mission project.

After four years of study, Tina left Trinity College with a BS in Nursing and a BA in Elementary Education. She took her final vows with her mentor Archbishop Stephan Costello at St. Patrick's Cathedral in Dublin. All the excitement started the dancin'-at-the-crossroads, and the drinkin'-of-the-pints, both of which Tina participated in. Her reputation of hard work, diligence and sharp intellect already had the Irish religious community buzzing about her.

Tina began working fulltime in the Dublin Chancery Office where her efforts continued to be exemplary. Sister had been selling off outdated church, school and hospital properties throughout the diocese. She would then allocate the monies to begin replacing those buildings with badly needed new ones. Her work had a profound effect on the community as new construction started. Her efforts were duplicated throughout the country and, as new jobs were created, it gave hope and optimism to Ireland.

After nearly three years of so many positive changes, Christina was on top of the world. Then, one day, the 25 year old nun was working at her desk when a soft knock came at the door. Sister looked up and said, "Come in." To her complete and utter amazement a truly holy person appeared in the doorway. It was a nun, a perfectly beautiful Sister of God. It was Kitty. "Sister Tina, I have no appointment. May I speak with you?" Dumbfounded, Tina rose out of her chair and reached out to embrace Kitty. Kitty could feel Tina's inner strength from their embrace. Sister knew the young lady would be a great Blessed-Sister.

"Sister, I spoke with Archbishop Costello. I wanted his permission to speak with you to discuss a proposal regarding your future." Tina replied, "Thank you Sister Kitty. Please feel free to speak your mind." The two women sat down and began to discuss the African Project and the Tanzanian Mission team. The discussion went on for several hours, working through lunch and finally stopping just before dinner. In the end, they were in near complete agreement. The only negotiated issue was that after the project was fully operational and stabilized, Tina would be allowed to leave to finish her work in Dublin. Kitty happily agreed to the terms thrilled that her Mission Team was now complete.

Tina said she needed a few weeks to tie up some loose ends before she could leave Dublin with a clear conscience. The Sisters hugged and agreed to meet on the Serengeti in 21 days.

* * * *

The four women began to settle in at the Mission, finding places for their teaching supplies and personal items. The Blessed-Sisters would accept all children between the ages of 6 and 13 into the program. They would be taught, loved, guided and prepared for life. The Sisters were also nurses so regular physical check-ups – especially vaccinations and understanding their bodies – were also part of the Sisters' vast itinerary. Each Blessed-Sister would have between 8 and 12 students to work with. Sister Gemma would have the youngest group, the 6 and 7 year olds. Sister Mira took the 8's and 9's, while Sister Tina was given the 10's and 11's. Kitty was happy to work with the older and more rambunctious 12 and 13 year olds.

Acclimating to life in the African jungle they would wait for the tribe's teen boys and elders to pass by on their hunt and then on their return trip home in the evening. The Blessed-Sisters knew that the entire tribe was excited about the Mission and wanted to spend time getting to know Wigo Nato's four newest members.

While all the Blessed-Sisters smiled and waved at the men, Kitty noticed that Gemma would continue to gaze in the direction the men had taken long after they were gone. Kitty knew that Gemma was a brilliant teacher but sensed she was fighting against her inner feelings about male relationships. Reverend Mother Kitty decided she would not broach the issue right now, not when the Mission was almost ready to open its doors. She would keep a close eye on the problem, fervently praying that Gemma would adjust to a nun's way of life.

The four women worked tirelessly to divide the responsibilities between themselves for such a multifaceted project. Each nun taught the others her area of expertise so everyone was able to cover the duties for each other if need be.

WELCOME!

It took six exhaustive weeks of preparation before they would be ready to meet the children. But the special day finally came as the Blessed-Sisters awaited the arrival of the students for their first day of school. The Sisters could hear the tribesmen singing off in the distance. The ladies' anticipation grew as the singing got closer. The children arrived hidden inside a protective circle of very skilled hunters. A large meat-eating animal will challenge just about anything but will keep their distance from a human group. The animals were cautious for good reason, humans are killers. As a group the tribesmen do not fear the predatory animals they hunt, however, they do fear for the safety of the women and children.

The tribesmen dropped the children off inside the gate and waved goodbye. Sister Kitty closed the large main gate which was wired to a separate electrical security system. With that system, the main gate could be opened without shutting down the compound's entire protective power source.

Kitty locked the gate and reconnected its alarm. The other Blessed-Sisters were leading the children to their proper classrooms. They were all a little shy but, at the same time, very excited for this new adventure to begin. The threats to behave from their mothers were taken seriously. All four Sisters were ecstatic, they were about to become *real* teachers in a faraway part of the world. They would teach reading, writing, math, science and the Word of God.

As a way of thanking the nuns, the mothers had made lunch for all 44 students and teachers. It was local cuisine: assorted berries, salted water buffalo meat and nuts. The Sisters supplied water, milk and cookies. They also had several sets of boy and girl clothing for emergencies. So as not to place the young ones under any undue pressure, the Sisters decided to wait on administering the vaccinations and giving out too much homework. Instead the focus was placed on song, fellowship and prayer.

Each Sister took one of the four large rooms in the building for her learning area. Gemma's style of teaching took the youngest group on a daily journey through time and space. It was as if she was an actress on stage, drawing her children into each performance. Working with only a few props and costumes, she could instantly transform herself into a witch, a wolf or an angel. Kitty would observe Gemma and beam with pride at her skills and the extent of her talent.

Mira's methods were far different as her students were a bit older, more educated and quieter. These students loved to study and learn. Sister Mira clearly understood the needs of her students allowing them to venture out into the water, but not too far.

As prepubescents, Tina's group was a year or so away from big changes – physiological ones. The children were smart and ready for more thought provoking studies and abstracts. Tina was a brilliant student herself which allowed her to encourage her group to stretch their minds and embrace the wonders of learning.

Finally, Kitty had the older children, 12 and 13 year olds. At this age they had learned enough from their elders to be able to speak English fluently. This gave Sister plenty of room to allow them to express themselves verbally, or by the written word. Some would even volunteer to be teacher assistants to help the younger children. Kitty had several of her students supervise the homework of the youngsters when they were back in their village and the idea had proved to be very effective. Kitty was hopeful that one day, one of her students would become a teacher or even a Blessed-Sister.

Sister Kitty, of course, had to keep an eye on everything. Most days she was thrilled with the results of the daily classes. After the children left for the day the four nuns would talk. 'What happened that day? What was planned for tomorrow? And, were they on schedule to reach their projected goals?' Several times a week, she would talk to each Sister individually. These discussions were more personal in nature and Kitty expected only a truthful accounting of their feelings.

Kitty gave more time to Gemma than the others, not because of favoritism but because she needed it. The young teacher had a not-so-secret secret which would have to be addressed soon. Sister had given the problem every chance to resolve itself but it hadn't. Now a heart to heart was needed; it was time for her "secret" to be discussed openly.

Kitty had just removed her slippers and was about to soak her tired feet. She had developed an after-hours routine where she would go outside the gates to feed the animals their leftovers. She would pet the lions, tigers and hyenas. Sister let them know that they too were God's creations and made valuable contributions to this world. In turn, they'd purr and lick Kitty's face and hands. The animals wouldn't fight with each other in her presence. Instead, they would parade around Sister, patiently waiting their turn to receive her touch.

Kitty looked forward to stepping into the bucket of warm water. To her surprise there was a light knock at her door and a voice spoke. "Reverend Mother, are you still up?" Sister answered, "Yes, please Gem, come in." Gemma apologized for the late hour and knelt down next to the bucket. She took the washcloth and began to wash Sister's feet. Kitty said "I'm glad you're here, I want to speak with you. But please, you first, tell me what *you* wanted to talk about."

"Sister, sometimes I see the older boys and I wish one of them would sneak into my room. The longing gets so bad that I begin to live in my imagination and it leads to me touching myself. The worst is that I no longer feel guilty. I can't get right. I keep saying that *this* will be the last time but I know it's a lie."

Kitty was listening intently and becoming very sympathetic to Gemma's situation. Before Kitty could express her feelings, Gemma had washed her hands up Sister's legs. Kitty had been so engrossed with Gemma's openness that she didn't realize that Gem had actually reached her upper thigh. Gemma had finally lost her battle with the need for physical contact. She was, ostensibly, trying to arouse her Reverend Mother.

She and Kitty were close in age being just six years apart. Gemma hoped that Sister might want to engage in some sort of physical contact. An angel, in human skin, *can* be tempted by sins of the flesh as well as any of the other seven deadly sins. Kitty instinctively reacted. She grabbed Gemma by the hair while tugging her up on the bed. As she half rose from the bed and reared back to slap her across the face, Kitty caught a flicker of darkness reflected in the mirror hanging on the wall just above her bureau. In that instant, in that tiny sliver of time, Kitty realized what had happened. She quickly pulled Gemma into her body and fiercely hugged her, instinctively protecting her from the evil that threatened to permeate her very soul.

The abrupt action by Kitty was enough to bring Gemma out of her fugue state. Having no knowledge or recollection of what had just occurred, Gemma sensed the discord in the room but incorrectly assumed it was Kitty's reaction to her earlier confession. "Kitty, I'm *so* sorry. How you must hate me now!" She tried to get up but Kitty refused to let her go. Shielding her further from evil, Kitty did not tell Gemma what had really happened. Instead she whispered, "Much of this is *my* fault. I knew you've been struggling with this problem for a while now and I've waited too long to discuss it with you. You are a fantastic teacher and *that* is your true calling. Unfortunately, you're in conflict with yourself. Your body and feelings have told you that you need a companion. A husband. You don't have to be a cloistered nun to teach or to do God's work. If you pray and ask God to help you, He will answer. His Grace is there for the asking. You need to be in front of children as God has blessed you with this talent. Please! *Forgive yourself for being human.*" Gemma was already relieved. She stayed, hugging Kitty for a while longer, very grateful for Sister's sage advice and understanding.

Gemma dozed off with her head still resting against her Reverend Mother's bosom. It was the first time since she arrived in Africa that she slept soundly, no longer burdened by her secret. Kitty began to fall asleep too, happy for her sister. She softly said, "Thank you, Lord."

Although Kitty was elated about the Mission's success, something still weighed heavily in her heart. The Devil's message had been loud and clear: He lurks in the African jungle. The next morning Kitty wrote a letter to Reverend Mother Pia explaining what had happened with her ward and recommended she be relocated someplace closer to Paris or New York as a civilian teacher.

The way Reverend Mother Pia handled the Gemma problem was brilliant. She felt that the loss of such a talented teacher would set the Mission back too far as it would take quite some time to find a suitable replacement. So Reverend Mother had called the Jesuits for help. They still had a small church in Tanzinato with five enclosed rooms in the church's basement. The rooms were primarily used to house displaced families but Pia asked if her daughter, Gemma, could stay there on weekends until other arrangements could be made. Gemma would be able to socialize, make friends and pursue relationships. She would live at the Mission during the week and commute to Tanzinato on Friday and back to the Mission early Monday morning. Reverend Mother Pia would also allow Gemma to keep her Blessed-Sister title to both the utter disbelief and complete delight of nuns and women all over the world.

With those arrangements in place, a new friend, Annamarie, told Gemma that she had someone she wanted her to meet. Robert Miller had been studying elementary education in his last year of seminary school, when, just before his final vows, his Rector asked him to take some time away from the priesthood to make sure it was still a clear path for him. Admittedly, his commitment to celibacy was becoming a problem. The Jesuits have always vetted their candidates very carefully as their priests live in remote and hostile places. They are alone for long stretches of time and have to be ready to move at a moment's notice.

Robert's evaluations were all the same: Great teaching skills – vast intelligence – super person – not meant for the priesthood. Like Gemma, he too stayed in Africa to help wherever he could. Unlike Gemma, he was not allowed to stay with his Order. Their relationship sparked. They had found love and fulfillment in each other's company. Within the year they were married.

Reverend Mother Pia was on top of things; she had a plan. She knew the Mission was doing great work and it was much stronger with Gemma aboard. At the same time, the Mission itself needed to be expanded and more teachers would have to be hired. Her solution was to erect a second floor above the Mission, update and increase the water, septic and storage systems and build an outdoor amphitheater for special events. She hired Robert as a guidance counselor and teacher. A new lay teacher, Ms. Gloria Edwards, was brought in to teach music and assist with the younger children.

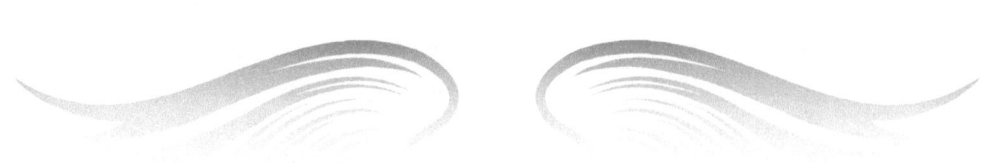

TEN YEARS AFTER

As a brutal and bloody civil war raged on an even deadlier force gripped the Dark Continent. The AIDS virus had taken hold, spreading rampantly across all of Africa. Death, destruction and despair. No one was spared its devastating effects.

The northwestern part of Tanzania saw many Rwandan Tutsis and Hutus escape across the border seeking asylum at any town or village that would take them in. The ravages of war, genocide and a pandemic had sent them quite literally running for their lives. It was a desperate time for the fleeing insurgents and a dangerous time for Tanzanians.

This upheaval presented the perfect opportunity for Hutu fanatics to purge the world of innocent prey. Defenseless scores of lost people could be found wandering the jungle roads. Much like America's own Civil War when slaves were set free after being released from southern plantations with no place to go. The Ku Klux Klan would savagely beat, rape, lash and murder these lost souls and go virtually unpunished for their deeds.

One of the very few positive elements in this ravaged nation was the Grace of God and the keys to knowledge brought to Africa by the Blessed-Sisters. The determination of the Blessed-Sisters to continue to teach and shelter all those who came to them during these tumultuous years gave peace and hope to hundreds.

Ten years had quickly passed them by. Some of their former students were now in their early twenties. The Blessed-Sisters and their Reverend Mother were a little weathered from a decade of hard work. Some had caught malaria. One had an emergency appendectomy. All had either family and/or friends pass away. The harsh realities of the world were stoically endured by four little Women of God. They were thousands of miles away from their native lands yet they only traveled 30 miles round trip to Tanzinato and back to the Mission which was now their home.

They had met the new millennium head on. Having reached 2004, Reverend Mother Kitty and her three missionaries, Gemma, Mira and Tina were a family. Each night the blank pages of their personal journals were happily filled with detailed entries for their own enjoyment and for future novices and postulants to learn from. The Sisters would look forward to reading one another's literary contributions on the weekends. On Sunday's they would look back at those precious moments and discuss each other's recordings.

From a relatively small Mission consisting of three women and one angel, major advancements in teaching methods and applications were being carved out. So much so that copies of each month's four journal entries were sent to the Paris Novitiate. The Mission team would wait like children on Christmas morning to hear back from Mother Pia. Pia's comments always began with "What a Blessing!" to the absolute delight of her charges.

* * * *

Ever since the renovations were completed eight years ago, the compound seemed to come alive. By expanding the Mission, Kitty had the room to hire daytime lay teachers to supplement her staff. It also freed Kitty to leave the compound on occasion to help oversee the progress of the other Mission sites that were under construction in Tanzania.

Sister knew that the Vatican was watching the Tanzanian Projects. Accurate reporting on their progress was mandatory. Pia had written asking for construction funds from the Supreme Tribunal of the Apostalic Signatura, the Vatican's most powerful court. She signed the letter, as did Jesuit Cardinal Campo and her old friend Mother Teresa.

The Blessed Sisters were now working on their 7th instructional book. The other two Missions were also operating at incredibly high levels. The students and their respective villages were eagerly discovering the power of knowledge, and the wonderment of Jesus.

The four Blessed-Sister's had endured almost ten years of trials and tribulations. For Gemma, life was perfect. For the other two nuns, they relished being in God's blessings. Robert felt everything was wonderful. He became the older brother to all the women in the Mission. Gloria Edwards, who took up residence in the last empty bedroom in the Mission was the Music Director. She had thought her life was over after the death of her husband several years before. The Wiga Nato Mission served as a new beginning for her. It recharged her life. Living in Africa provided a spectacular backdrop in fulfilling her life's dream; teaching children the wonder and joy of music. She felt that bringing God and knowledge to its children would bring the light to the Dark Continent. What Gloria didn't expect was that it also brought the light back into her heart.

* * * *

As the 10th Annual Christmas Talent Show approached, everyone was making preparations to make this year's show better than those preceding it. It would be a major accomplishment as each year the shows were deemed better than the prior year's performance. Questions swirled around the compound: Could this year's show really top last year's show? Could Gloria bring fresh new acts to the performance? And, was Blessed-Sister Gemma with child? Only three people, other than Gemma herself, knew that she was. One was her husband Robert, another was Kitty and the third was Reverend Mother Pia. Pia thought it was 'about damned time' that a *married* nun could actually give birth with the church's blessing. Sisters of the Church from all over the world awaited word from Wiga Nato.

The school children took home flyers that said:

December 22, 2004
THE 10*th* ANNUAL WIGA NATO MISSION
HOLIDAY TALENT SHOW
ALL ARE INVITED

* * * *

At the end of the day, the efforts of the 10th Annual Talent Show had surpassed last year's show. The kids were serious about making it the best. They were all excellent students regarding academics, special activities, and spiritual studies. They embraced anything that could be learned. The

Blessed-Sisters, along with Gloria and Robert, were firing on all cylinders. The day had been incredible. However, as always, it was near sundown and they had to send everyone back, lay teachers included, to their respective villages. The night belonged to the predators. Predators instinctively know how to kill at night when the sun is down – with stealth – and with the element of surprise. The fearless tribesmen would be overmatched trying to protect so many women and young children.

The Blessed-Sisters vowed to clean up that night even though they were exhausted. Their years in the Novitiate had ingrained upon them a very rigid, organized schedule which ultimately served them well in Africa. Tonight, however, it served them with mops and brooms and stacks of dirty dishes. Tomorrow would be a well-deserved day off for the Blessed-Sisters and if they handled the mess now they could sleep in for most of the day.

Bone tired and barely keeping her eyes open, Gemma realized a moment too late that she walked straight into the forward motion of Mira and a soggy, soapy mop. Beyond tired, Mira started giggling and was soon joined by Gemma, Tina and Kitty. The slap happy Sisters finished the clean-up with three broken dishes, six bags of garbage and one very clean pair of shoes.

At this point they were so *over*tired they made a pot of tea and relaxed around the large kitchen table. Quietly sipping tea they were each lost in their own thoughts when a sudden noise startled them out of their reveries. The Sisters became fully alert at the sound of a creaking door. *Something* or someone was coming out of Kitty's room and it was coming towards them.

Sister Mira carried a gun in a shoulder holster. She had asked permission to carry a weapon in the evenings and near her bed after lights-out. Sister Mira was deathly afraid of animals and had learned how to handle small firearms as a child in Brazil. No one had the heart to tell her that her 22 caliber Smith and Wesson would be very ineffective against large African animals. It made Mira feel safe so Kitty allowed it with one proviso: "Be *very* careful."

All eyes were on Kitty's door as Mira drew her sidearm from her holster vest. The door continued to open and in the dark of the room they could see two eyes low to the ground. "Reverend Mother, should I shoot?" whispered Mira. "No!" Kitty whispered back, "I don't think it's an animal."

As they stared at the doorway to Kitty's room, a dark shadow flashed in the doorway. Mira gasped, then heaved a great sigh of relief. A baby was crawling out of Kitty's room. "Oh no," said Kitty. "That's Wykeena's youngest sister. She was at the party and evidently found her way into my room for a nap." Because of all the activities of the day her absence had gone unnoticed. "Gem," said Kitty, "Go over and let her know we're happy to see her. Then change her diaper and wash her up." Gemma was the perfect person for the job, showering the child with love and attention. Mira was sent to warm up the truck and bring it around front. Gloria and Robert had taken the other pick-up truck to Tanzinato with a list of basics that the Mission needed to get through New Year's week. Tina was setting the gate's electric override. It had to be done quickly; the Mission had to be kept safe.

Kitty knew that the villagers must be going crazy searching high and low for the missing little girl. The only answer was for Kitty to drive the child back *tonight*. The Blessed-Sisters made everything ready for the emergency trip into the African darkness.

The ride to the Wiga Nato village was only 2 miles north of the Mission. But the ride would be on a three-rut dirt lane and the night was pitch-black. On the plus side, large animals might stay near a vehicular road but rarely ventured onto it. Sister knew that a straight run was doable. There would be no other vehicles on the road at that hour.

The ride wasn't far but it was dangerous. It would be better if the toddler slept the whole way back to the village. As Gemma gently strapped the girl into the car seat, Tina covered her with a soft blanket and gave her a bottle of warm milk. Sucking contentedly, the little one drifted off into the peaceful sleep of the innocent.

Kitty jumped into the driver's seat and told her Blessed-Sisters that she'd be back in 30 minutes. And, if not, they should all go to bed. "When I get back, I'll blow the horn to scare anything away." Just before they pulled away, Mira insisted that Kitty take the handgun. Just in case.

When she pulled into the village 15 minutes later, she found the entire tribe on Red Alert. When they realized it was sister Kitty with the missing child they were relieved. They had already killed three animals, a lioness and two hyenas, and cut their stomachs open to check for contents. Again the village showed Kitty their unwavering love and appreciation for bringing her back safe and sound. Kitty prayed the whole way back thanking God for His Mercy.

    She couldn't wait to get back to let the Sisters know everything was fine. As Kitty pulled up to the Mission gates, she could see that the high-voltage lights were out. She had been struggling to bring forth a thought that was floating at the edge of her memory. Then she remembered — *the haunting spector* that had appeared in her mirror ten years before. The hairs on the back of her neck stood up. Something was terribly wrong. Where were her Blessed-Sisters? Fighting off panic, Kitty got out of the SUV and approached the now eerily silent compound.

THE AFRICAN OUTRAGE

Shortly after Kitty left, her three exhausted Blessed-Sisters made their way back into the kitchen area and settled in at the large wooden discussion table to await her safe return. After about 20 minutes of quietly rehashing the night's turn of events, another noise startled them. Looking at each other quizzically, Sister Tina was the first to speak, "Oh no, not another child?" Turning their heads in unison toward the sound the three Blessed-Sisters were rendered speechless at the sight of two large rebel soldiers dressed for guerilla warfare. Warfare had taught them many survival skills. One such skill was: how to short circuit an electrified fence. Then lying in wait until it was time to strike.

Again, it was Tina who found her voice first. "Who are you and what brings you here to our Mission?" she asked. "Come here, all of you!" screamed Sladuu, the larger and obvious leader of the two. The Blessed-Sisters shakily moved around the table, instinctively raising their arms half-way with palms up, showing they were no threat to these two warriors. Motioning with his rifle Sladuu barked another command, "Away from the table. Over here, NOW!" Gemma and Mira quickly ran toward Sister Tina. The group of three were scared out of their minds and looking for strength and comfort from one another.

Like all experienced soldiers they were on top of their prey before the Sisters could react. With AK-47s pointed at their heads, the Sisters were ordered to remove all of their clothing. Mira screamed in fear and was rewarded with the butt end of his rifle being slammed into the back of her head. It would come to be a death blow. Thinking only of her unborn child, Gemma started to run but was viciously yanked back into the room as if she was nothing more than a rag doll.

Tina stared in shock as the second warrior, Naapu, threw Mira on top of the table, tore off the nun's clothes, and began examining her vaginal area. They were searching for virgins – women who couldn't have contracted the AIDS (HIV) virus from sexual intercourse. And the best place to find one was in a convent. Satisfied that the young nun was pure, Naapu quickly discarded his fatigues and thrust himself into an unconscious Mira.

The Sisters could have never prepared for the violence these two soldiers were about to unleash upon them. They had either been banished or rejected from every tribal village in a 200 mile radius of Wiga Nato. True sociopaths, they were unable to live in communities with other human beings. A dispute with an unsuspecting neighbor tribesman could result in one of his younger children being lured into the bush where the child would be bound and gagged and left as food for the night predators.

Sladuu and Naapu were especially fond of raping teenaged girls. They relished tearing the vaginal opening in horrendously painful ways. One survivor hauntingly recalled the night it happened to her. "The big one, he keep bitin' me on the inside of my thighs. I scream and scream, it hurts so bad! Bad man keep laughin' and bitin' harder. The little one, he grab me by the ankles and pull my legs apart so wide I think I break in two. Then the big one, oh God, the big one he bite me *there*! Then he takes his fist and punches it. Again and again and again, all the while crazy laughin'. I can't take no more! I beggin' him to stop but he don't. He climb on top and sticks his thing into me an' I try to scream but I don't got no air, he stranglin' me while he do his business in me. I close my eyes and I pray to God to take me. Just take me Lord, take me now. But He must not a' heard me cause the big one finished and let go my neck. I open my eyes and he standing over me, licking my blood off his fingers. Now the little one is laughin' too, just like a human hyena. It was his turn…"

* * * *

Sladuu hit Gemma repeatedly in the head, legs and belly. He shoved her down onto the table and violently tore off her clothes. But when he saw Gemma's naked body he stopped cold. She was with child. Enraged, Sladuu grasped Gemma's head with his hands and banged it on the table over and over again, literally beaten into a shapeless mass. Letting go in disgust at her perceived betrayal, he turned his attention to Tina who screamed out in terror. She was immediately punished with a vicious thrust to the ribs with the blunt end of his rifle, breaking several bones. Unleashing a maniacal cackle, he grabbed Tina around her broken ribcage and slammed her body down onto the table between Gemma on his right and Mira on his left.

Sladuu seized Tina's ankles and began positioning her body on the edge of the table. In agony, Sister was begging for mercy. In response, he silenced her with a punch delivered directly under her heart. Tina went limp, unable to catch her breath. Straddling the nearly unconscious nun, Sladuu rammed his entire member into her in one violent motion.

Just then, a vehicle drove up to the compound's front gates. Kitty had returned.

* * * *

Pulling up to the compound, Kitty felt that something wasn't quite right. Sitting in the truck for a moment she suddenly realized that the blinking red lights indicating power to the gates were not on. Kitty was worried. Was it possible that the compound had been breached or was she just overreacting? Then she noticed sparks intermittently shoot out from behind the amphitheater at the north end of the compound. Now Sister was afraid. Having no other choice, she reached into the glove compartment and grabbed Sister Mira's handgun. Instead of rejoicing with her Blessed-Sisters about the successful return of the little girl, she was carrying a sidearm into the Mission. For what, she did not yet know.

As she tiptoed inside, Kitty faced the worst of her fears. Splayed out before her were her beloved Blessed-Sisters, battered beyond recognition on the large discussion table. Tina was begging her attackers to stop, but her words were garbled because she was so badly beaten. Kitty walked in on Sladuu yanking Tina down to the edge of the table by her ankles.

For Kitty it was like being frozen in a real, live nightmare, one that you can never wake up from. It was evil at its most profound. Drawing a breath so deep it seemed to come from the very depths of her soul, Kitty shouted, "STOP!" Startled, both men turned and looked over their shoulders to find Sister Kitty pointing a gun at them. They both reached for their weapons. Again, Sister warned them. "Do not move or I *will* shoot!" Both men ignored her threat and began to turn with their guns held high and ready to shoot. Kitty shot them both.

Dropping the gun, Kitty ran to Gemma first. She felt no heartbeats from either Gemma or the baby. Sister moved over to Mira. She too was terribly beaten and mortally wounded.

As Kitty reached Tina, the nun opened her swollen eyes and spoke. Sister jumped on the table and placed her ear next to Tina's mouth. She began to speak in whispers of air, "I – love – you – Reverend – Mother – and – my – Sisters. Thank – you – for – everyth . . . ."

Kitty cried as Tina's words tailed off but Sister had clearly received her message. It was as if she postponed her death and held on just to say thanks. Overcome with loss, Kitty was near hysteria. The three people she loved as her family were gone. Sister was forced to pull herself together because she had to move quickly. Danger could come from anywhere. Kitty had to get out of her emotional state and allow her intellect to take over.

* * * *

There were large predators nearby and, while friendly to Kitty, they would soon be overcome by the smell of blood from the five dead bodies. To complicate matters, the two men bore the body markings of a fighting unit which was known to be very aggressive. Kitty didn't know if other soldiers would come looking for them when they did not return to their camp by morning. Even these two soldiers could touch off an unjust war if their bodies were discovered with bullet holes in them.

Sister ran outside and backed the truck up to the front steps. As gently as she could, she dragged the bodies of her three Sisters out to the truck and placed them into the cargo area. She then went back inside to examine the bodies of the two men. Once she confirmed that they too were dead, Sister dragged them outside, down the steps and out beyond the gate. Sister knew enough to bring the bodies of the two men into the jungle where their remains would be eaten by wild animals. Fittingly, the first to pounce were the hyenas.

Kitty had just two more orders of business before she could leave the area. First, she grabbed the satchel that had the last several chapters of book

#7. Sister thought, "This work, along with the other six volumes, will be my Blessed-Sisters' legacy to children all over the world." Her second duty was to burn down the mission because a sacred building must be purged from mortal sin before it can again be used for God's work. Fire is an extreme and powerful form of purification.

Kitty started a controlled fire designed to burn down the Mission but would not explode the underground gas tanks. Turning over barrels of rainwater she flooded the back area outside the gates where the tanks were buried and covered the two fill spouts inside the gates with water-soaked canvas and stones. Finally, Kitty started a fire with the shredded clothing of the Blessed-Sisters and some flammable kitchen cleaners.

Kitty jumped in the truck and pulled away, heartbroken and in disbelief. Her large animal friends ran along on either side of the truck to protect their angelic friend and her special cargo. Then one by one the animals fell behind, leaving Kitty feeling empty and alone. Behind her she could see the flames spiraling up on a dark, windless night. Kitty's three Blessed-Sisters had been murdered, she killed two men, and the Mission was gone.

* * * *

Back home in France, Kitty seemed lost. She was deeply ashamed about all that had happened in Africa and therefore felt she could not turn to the Lord for help. Sister would spend her days crying in the novitiate's cemetery, tenderly caring for the flowers she planted on the graves of her three Blessed-Sisters and unborn brother. Eventually, she became numb inside, protecting herself against the pain that was lodged deep within her heart. Feeling neither joy nor sorrow, Kitty was trapped inside her own little world, not living but merely existing.

She mistook Pia's reserved demeanor as both judgement and punishment for her unbearable failure to protect her Blessed-Sisters at Wiga Nato. Believing that she had already lost her God and now her Reverend Mother tormented Kitty during every waking hour. She was grieving not only for her Blessed-Sisters but for the loss of Pia's friendship as well.

Wracked with pain both physically and mentally, Kitty was quickly plummeting into the desolate pit of hopeless despair. As she was tending to the convent garden on one particularly warm summer morning, Kitty suddenly thought of her father. He had always been so easy to talk to and was her rock while she was growing up. Thinking about her father naturally brought on thoughts of her departed mother. Kitty's mother had died during the terrorist attack at the World Trade Center in New York on September 11, 2001. For the first time in months, Kitty knew what she had to do.

Walking purposefully into the convent, Sister Kitty hesitated briefly outside Reverend Mother Pia's office before softly knocking on the door. She was immediately ushered in by Pia herself and invited to join her for a latte and croissant, a Parisian indulgence that they both enjoyed immensely.

Sensing Kitty's discomfort, Reverend Mother tried to put her at ease by saying, "I'm delighted you stopped by to see me! It's been a very long time since we've talked and I miss you Kitty." "You *missed* me?" asked Kitty. Confused, Pia replied, "Of course I did. Why would you think any differently?" The sudden realization that she hadn't lost her Reverend Mother at all was such an enormous relief that Kitty crumbled and wept. She wept for her losses and she wept for the joy of having the unwavering love and support of a woman who meant the world to her.

Reverend Mother stood quietly by Kitty's side with her hand on her shoulder, giving her time to release the emotions that had been bottled up for far too long. When Sister Kitty could speak again, she told Pia about her plans to visit her father and honor her mother by praying for her and the other lost souls at Ground Zero. Pia wrapped her arms in a protective fold around her beloved angel and whispered, "Go with God."

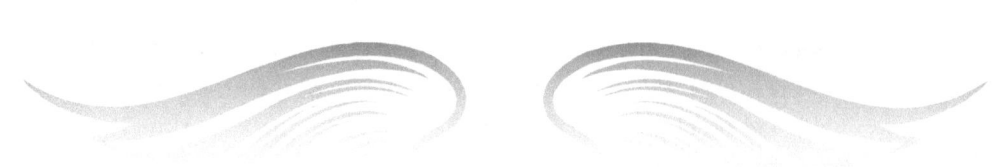

DAD'S OFFICE

Sister Kitty McGuire was on a plane heading toward America. Her Reverend Mother had supported her decision to go back to New Jersey to visit the place where she had lived for 11 years. She agreed that Kitty needed a change of venue and going home just might be the cure.

Kitty had been lost, despondent and unable to come to terms with the horrific tragedy that occurred six months earlier. As she hoped it would, the plane ride offered a nice diversion to her drifting thoughts and sadness. Kitty allowed herself the luxury of interacting with people and, for the first time in months, she began to feel alive again.

No matter where she was, children would first stare and then gravitate over to Kitty just to be near her. This loving attention was always reciprocated with smiles and hugs. Some said that children can see a light around her. A halo. Others said it was an aura. Whatever it was, it made Kitty happy.

Just as the sun was rising, the plane reached America's northeast coastline. Kitty could see the empty space where the Twin Towers and seven other buildings had once proudly stood. The entire area, once so powerful, had been reduced to rubble, a grim reminder that evil does exist.

After arriving at Newark Airport in New Jersey, Kitty jumped on a NJ Transit train and headed for her childhood home which was only an hour away. Sister desperately needed to see Plains where she had grown up with her adoptive parents. Later she'd take the train back up to her Dad's office in New York City with an ETA of 11:00 a.m.

David and Marie Amico were Kitty's next door neighbors and friends. David, who was simply called Sheriff by everyone and his wife had looked after her whenever her parents, John and Carol, needed to work late. As she got older they were always there for help and guidance. She loved them like they were her second set of parents. Kitty also loved their eight hunting dogs. They had no children of their own so they treasured the time they spent with Sister.

On this day, Sheriff and Marie were eating breakfast together at home. Out of the picture window overlooking their side yard, something caught Marie's eye. "Honey, I just saw a woman get out of a cab and walk straight into John's house." "You sure?" Sheriff asked. "Yeah," said Marie. They both stood and continued to observe from the window.

About 250' separated their home from the McGuire's. The property line was blurred many years ago and Kitty had used the entire area as her playground. The grounds were flat with plush green grass and elevated trees. About 30' out from John's house was a natural low spot. It would catch rain water which would settle at the depth of the grass. It was a breeding ground for tree frogs, roly-polies and large Jersey mosquitoes. As a child Kitty thought it was the greatest place on Earth. Now she longed to squish her toes in the wet grass and splash around like she used to.

Kitty's father and Uncle Sheriff grew up in Plains and were classmates and best friends all throughout grammar and high school. Sheriff and Marie had been both steadfast and tender when John's wife Carol was killed on 9/11. John often said that he didn't know where he'd be without his neighbors loving and consistent support.

Marie's eyes lit up. She, in her Texas drawl said, "Hey Dave, look who it is and she all grown-up!" Sheriff was in shock, "The dogs know who it is; look at them run! God, she's beautiful." The couple ran over, thrilled to see Kitty once again after all these years.

The dogs were fighting each other just to lick Sister's face. The splashing turned the little puddle into a liquid mosh pit. Kitty's laughter could clearly be heard from the middle of the raucous scrum. When Sister saw her friends approaching she jumped up and shouted, "Marie! Sheriff! It's me, Kitty!" Sheriff and his wife wrapped their arms around their beautiful, exuberant "niece."

The three obviously loved each other. They hugged and cried with the happiness of being together again. Kitty broke the moment by saying she had to catch the 9:00 a.m. train to NYC to see her father. Sheriff offered to drive Kitty to New York but Kitty said, "Uncle Sheriff if you and Marie could drive me to the train station in Princeton, it would be perfect."

* * * *

After what seemed like an eternity, Kitty finally arrived at her father's office. As she walked down the long corridor she remembered running down this same hallway as a seven-year-old. Sister saw an open door which she knew led to the large conference room, the one with the big chairs that you could sit in and spin around on. As she got closer to the room she could clearly hear her dad's strong, confident voice; the voice she hadn't heard for more than 10 years.

Kitty slowed as she reached the conference room, overwhelmed by the thought that soon she would be able to see the man she loved so very much. As she leaned around the door jamb and poked her head in, Sister realized that she was only a couple of feet behind her father. He couldn't see her but the 12 people who sat around the large conference table could and were openly distracted by her presence. John stopped speaking as he realized that no one was listening and seemed to be looking at something behind him. He turned around to see what was going on but no one was there. Kitty had decided to go through the receiving area so as not to further disrupt the meeting. John turned back to ask his dozen business associates what they had been looking at. One man spoke up and said, "It was a beautiful Chinese woman." Everyone at the table nodded in agreement. John rose from his seat to look up and down the hallway but saw no one.

Kitty was greeted by Joan, her dad's longtime office manager, who was stunned at Sister's transformation from schoolgirl to beautiful young woman of God. They hugged and Joan said, "Kitty, it's so good to see you again!" She turned and gestured to a lovely young woman sitting at the adjacent desk. "Kitty, I want you to meet Mae. She's not much older than you but she's very special to your father." Kitty whispered out loud to Joan, "Wow, she really loves him." Shocked, Joan replied, "How on Earth did you know that?" Kitty answered, "He's in her heart." Sister gave Mae a hug, "I think it would be great if you married him." Mae and Joan both stared at her in awe.

After a few moments Joan told Sister that she had to go see her father right now. Kitty was concerned about disrupting his meeting but Joan said, "Don't worry about that. He really needs to see you. Let's not keep him waiting any longer."

All three ladies walked through John's office and into the conference room. Kitty just stood there for a moment, and then quietly said, "Daddy." John jumped up and with immense pride said, "Everyone, this beautiful young woman is not Chinese, she's Vietnamese and French." He choked back his tears, then announced, "And she's my daughter!"

Father and daughter briskly moved around to the head of the table where they hugged and openly wept with joy. Holding her hands John said, "Kitty, you're just in time to join us for a small brunch that we have set up across the street." One of the men said, "No John, you need to spend time alone with your daughter." Everyone gathered their things and began to file out happily as they had just witnessed a beautiful reunion.

"Daddy, I need to speak with you about so many things," stated Kitty. "Like what happened in Africa, your beautiful friend Mae and your new son…" John spoke loudly interrupting his daughter, "And my new what?" "Oh sorry," said Kitty. "You didn't know? Well, he already loves you." John looked shocked. He was not aware of Mae's pregnancy. "Boy Kit, you really can stir things up."

"Dad, I have to go to *Ground Zero* and make peace with what happened to Mom," said Kitty. Her father nodded his head and said, "I understand honey. Do you want me to go with you?" "No Dad, it's something I have to do by myself. I also have to stop on the Upper West Side to speak with the mother of one of my missionary Sister's from Africa."

Father and daughter hugged once again and Kitty said she hoped to be back in two hours. John told her to start heading downstairs where he'd send a cab to meet her right away. After one more hug Sister said, "I'll see you right after I'm done with my appointments." With that, Kitty smiled and took her leave.

GROUND ZERO

Sister Kitty got out of the cab amazed at the emptiness of her surroundings. Both towers and many other structures were missing from the site she remembered so vividly from her early teens. "The smallness," she recalled. How very small she felt looking straight up for 1,000 feet; and how ingenious humanity had become erecting buildings that seemed to touch the sky. The concrete and steel buildings had always seemed so permanent to her. Then, on one fateful day, they crashed and burned, killing thousands of innocent people. For a while, she just stood and stared, literally frozen in her sadness.

Kitty had been stationed half way around the world at the Wiga Nato Mission in Africa during the 9/11 attacks. However, on that evening, she sensed something bad had happened. There was an ominous feeling that drifted through the air. Tragically, Kitty's instincts were correct as her mother, Carol, had been senselessly killed. Several weeks later, word was sent by courier confirming her worst fears. The message also contained a plea from her father that she *not* come back to America. Her mother's remains had never been recovered, but a memorial service was held and a beautiful granite cross marked the place where an empty casket was laid to rest. Her grieving father clearly conveyed that he desperately had to leave New Jersey for a while. John needed to escape from the painful images he had witnessed. He had always found comfort up at Lake Cayuga, one of New York State's Finger Lakes. He also wanted to get away from his business office in New York, which was located only a few blocks north of the World Trade Center.

John had only *heard* the first plane fly by his office but stared in horror as he saw the second plane hit the South Tower, knowing all too well that it was the building where his wife Carol was working. She was a United Nations tour guide. On that day, she and her group visiting from China had arrived at the World Trade Center promptly at 8:00 a.m. John said, "That second plane looked demonic. Its intentions were to do something beyond bad – something evil."

Kitty walked twenty paces to a steel railing where she could look down to see men working on a new building. She sat on a park bench and removed her brown leather flats and plain white cotton socks. She reached into her purse for her beige habit and placed it on her head. Sister then knelt on her bare knees, slightly leaning back on the heels of her feet. Placing her purse on the ground in front of her, she began to pray.

She prayed until the images appeared. Kitty could see her mother and the Chinese nationals having breakfast in the Sky Lobby on the 78th floor of the South Tower. All of Carol's guests from Hong Kong were completely enamored with the view, feeling the power and pulse of the city's streets that were 77 floors beneath them. Then, looking south over the harbor, a curious looking plane had caught Carol's eye. Through her mother's eyes, Kitty could see the plane too. It seemed to be picking up speed as it got closer. The group had already been alerted to an accident involving a small plane over at the North Tower earlier that morning. But the South Tower had been cleared of any danger. As she continued to monitor the situation, Carol realized that something was seriously wrong. Kitty was screaming at the image, "Run Mama, run away!" But it was as futile as yelling at the television during a sporting event.

Carol watched in disbelief, seeing the nose of the plane heading straight toward the 78th floor. She could see several men in the cockpit waving their arms in praise and cheering their own despicable actions. Kitty could feel her mother's fear and disbelief. The plane, now traveling at nearly six hundred miles per hour, struck. Her mother was gone.

It was extremely painful for Kitty. She began to break off her flashbacks but decided to stay in tune being meant to see all that happened on that horrific morning. Like rolling thunder, both towers were violently resurrected – twin volcanoes rising back into existence. Kitty found herself kneeling at the foot of an already burning North Tower. Her senses were instantly overloaded. There was cell phone chatter everywhere. Sirens screamed from all directions. Fire trucks, police cars and EMS vehicles were descending on the World Trade Center at breakneck speeds. The epicenter of something worse than an earthquake; someone had declared war on America. It was a deliberate disaster.

A blizzard of white office paper wafted down and covered the streets in a blanket of white. The scent of death was prevalent. While the message was loud and clear, the signals were poorly received. There was too much information to process which resulted in profound confusion. The one overwhelming reaction to the moment was stark fear. The disintegration of the Twin Towers was one of those rare moments in human history where a singular, sudden and shocking act had changed the world, only this time, it was for the worse.

Sister looked up to find dozens of people jumping out of their office windows. The hellish orange flames and endless billows of gray smoke seemed to be coaxing them to jump. Their bodies tumbled down through the air at two hundred miles per hour. The friction from the air speed tore off their shoes and skirts and jackets as they hurdled toward the Earth. The landings were sickening. No mercy. No exceptions. Some bodies crashed on top of the aluminum canopies hanging over the plaza. They made sharp, resonating sounds which violently shook the plaza's doors and windows. Others fell directly to the ground, literally exploding on impact, propelling arms and legs in all directions.

Each building collapsed faster than the speed of sound, creating a dark and massive smoke cloud that roared down city streets. The thick, acrid smoke enveloped everything in its path, chasing survivors away and cloaking a city in a thick layer of debris.

Fear caused total strangers to grasp each other in desperate need of someone to verify that they were still alive. Their primal instincts demanded they take flight from danger. They ran in blind panic, gulping for what little air was left in lower Manhattan. The attacking smoke cloud had caked their faces with white concrete powder, making it almost impossible to breathe. The runners' expressions turned to blank bewilderment. They were lost. It was perfect cruelty based on classical conditioning – run or die.

The tragedies at the Pentagon and in Pennsylvania were almost incomprehensible at that point; too much tragedy for the world to absorb in a single morning. The most profound visuals swirled around New York City. The world's greatest city looked beaten and shattered. Evil rejoiced, firmly embedding fear not only in the cracks and crevices of the sidewalks of NY, but in the heart and soul of a nation.

In a moment of clarity, Kitty realized, "If the terrorists really wanted to cripple the region's commerce, they could have attacked more strategic targets like the bridges and tunnels, isolating the island of Manhattan from the rest of the world. Instead, they deliberately chose something less tactical but more spectacular. They did so by preying on human emotions through the senses. By assailing people's sensibilities with pure terror, they assailed their human values. Their plan was ingenious, flawless and diabolical."

In addition to the towers, seven other buildings would fall on 9/11, continuing the nightmare well into the next day. With 21st century telecommunication technology, nothing in the history of the world compares to this one day of sheer visual horror. As each building fell, newscasters would report it with disbelief and dread, "Another building has fallen." People watching around the world became reluctant witnesses to the real-time television transmissions and frozen moments where time stood still. Those on site became unwitting actors portraying true terror. "Not in America!" they shouted. "Things like that don't happen here." Finally, Kitty shut off the images. She now fully understood that humanity had begun to implode. Sister began to openly weep as she continued to pray.

Later, Sister would note that the flashbacks were there, at Ground Zero, for anyone who needed to confront and come to terms with the things that happened and the events that hurt them so very much. Kitty said that if you lost a loved one there you could access, by prayer, what was seen through their eyes. But you would also experience their suffering. Sister wanted everyone to be aware of and prepare for what they would see, hear, touch, taste and smell. It was different for her. She knew what was to be expected and it was something she was obligated to do. It was extremely painful.

Sister was deep in prayer as a chartered bus pulled up to the curb. The passengers had all shifted over to the Ground Zero side of the bus. They were shocked to see a singular nun kneeling in prayer by the construction railing with a glow around her. Not all could see the glow but all twelve knew this person was special.

Kitty had lost track of time. She had one more appointment to make before she could go back to her dad's office. She slowly opened her eyes to find herself surrounded by twelve people. They too were praying while waiting for Sister to come out of her trance. To Kitty's surprise, one of them spoke up and said, "Sister, are you an angel?" Now Kitty was wide awake, "Why would you ask that? Are my wings showing?" Sister was being playful with her newfound admirers whom she realized were a group of very holy people.

They had come together, through Christ, by having lost loved ones in the attack on 9/11. Kitty stood up and wiped off her knees and the tops of her feet. She spoke to the twelve, "I'm forbidden to speak of it." Then she smiled. But they got it. Several of them actually collapsed to the ground, some clutched their chest and the others raised their arms in praise. Sister lightly admonished them saying, "Only God must be praised, never his servants." They all nodded in agreement fully understanding her message. However, they also knew God had answered their prayers. They had gotten the sign they had prayed for – God was there and He was watching.

Kitty knew her time was short and she still had one more stop to make. She explained that her mother had also died there on 9/11 and that she needed to grieve her loss. Sister asked the group, "Would you like to pray together? God loves when followers pray together." They all stood and formed a circle around the angel they had just met. Kitty put out both arms and invited them to touch her sleeves. One member of the group led them in the Our Father, Hail Mary and Glory Be. One of the men flagged a cab and paid the driver the fare for Sister's ride uptown. Kitty was so happy. The group continued to wave goodbye for blocks. Later on, a member shared that the moments with "their" angel were truly blissful.

THE UPPER WEST SIDE

The cab ride uptown to the west side of Central Park was exhilarating. So many cars, so many people and so many concrete buildings. The cabbie would swerve from one lane to another, constantly stopping and starting. It seemed like everyone in the world lived in New York and they all walked the streets and drove their cars at the same time of day.

The cabbie pulled up on the service entrance side of the building Kitty needed to visit. He said, "Sister, I'd rather leave you off here than see you have to wait for *them* to finish." The cabbie was pointing to the firemen on the corner where they were rolling hoses and cleaning their equipment in the street. Two large fire trucks were blocking the road. The cabbie said, "Sister, turn at the corner just past the firehouse, that's your building's main entrance. I'll be stuck here forever unless I leave now. Please go and get to your appointment on time. And Sister, please take the money that the guy at Ground Zero gave me for your fare. Let the ride be my gift to you." Kitty again was made to feel like she was delivering God's message. That people actually wanted to *believe*. These reactions were giving her the inner strength to carry on. Working for The Lord is wonderful but also can be so very challenging. That horrible night in Africa caused her to question her ability to serve. Her visit to America was beginning to help her restore her confidence in herself.

Kitty closed the cab's door and stepped up onto the sidewalk. She watched the taxi back out, then drive off. Sister continued down the street but an old woman beckoned her to the side entrance. It was actually the service entrance, which was about 50 ft. from the firehouse. The firehouse occupied the entire northwest corner and the two floors above it.

Kitty held up a piece of paper so the older woman could read it. "Yeah, yeah Mrs. O'Dwyer," she said in broken English, "Come in this way." Kitty stepped in through the doorway, where the area was dimly lit with flickering bulbs and was noticeably darker from the sun's blinding glare outside. It disoriented Sister and, after two small steps, a man stepped into Kitty's path and punched her in the pelvis, just above the genitalia. Sister fell to her knees clutching her abdomen in agony. The older woman came from behind and covered Sister's mouth and nose with a cloth soaked in chloroform. In seconds she went limp the way a marionette will collapse in a heap when the puppeteer drops its strings.

The delivery area was filthy, filled with garbage and discarded drug paraphernalia. The older couple began to work quickly. They lifted Sister off the grimy floor and onto a soiled cart which had been hidden behind a small pile of boxes. In a matter of seconds, they were on their way to the top floor via the service elevator. The trip going up would not be interrupted as the top three floors housed no tenants and the building was under renovation. There was simply no one there to see anything. The abduction of this beautiful young woman was completed in less than five minutes.

THE CRAZED MAN

While beating women, the crazed man would sometimes drift off into a dark place in his memory to a time when he was a child.

One evening, when he was seven, he had to go to the bathroom very badly. His problem was that the only bathroom in the two room attic apartment was on the far side of his mother's bedroom. To get to the bathroom he'd have to crawl through his mother's bedroom, tightly packed with chairs and an extra night table, and be as quiet as a mouse. Then he'd have to crawl out the same way he had come in – quietly. Worst of all, he couldn't flush the toilet because of the loud sound of cascading water which echoed throughout the apartment. This disturbance would alert his mother to the fact that he had been in her room. And that simply was not allowed.

At night, his mother would invite men, and sometimes women, over for an evening of *erotica*. She would bed a man both for money and to continue her search for the perfect relationship. On those nights when his mother was *busy*, Daniel was allowed to watch television well after his bedtime. It drowned out the moans and screams and all of the other sounds of sex. Sometimes the bedroom noises got so loud he'd have to bury his head under his pillow. Mostly, he managed. Except for the times when he'd have to go to the bathroom.

He had tried other ways to neatly relieve himself but they didn't work. Once he pooped into a coffee can and hid it on an outside window sill. The heat and humidity made it stink to high heaven before he could sneak it away from the apartment. Another time, he held it in all night but by morning it turned to water. The cramps made him explode diarrhea all over his p.j.'s, sheets and bed. In both cases his mother beat him and then forced him to clean up *his* messes. This further complicated matters because the odor of excrement made him queasy. He'd become sick to his stomach and was constantly weak from dehydration and exhaustion.

After all his mother's transactions were completed, there was usually a window of opportunity when they'd collapse together in a sweaty, sticky bedding puddle. It was then that he'd crawl through her bedroom, do his business, and get back into the living room without incident. The living room offered a small sanctuary for the boy. It had a couch and television in the center, and a fold-up bed in the far corner. It wasn't that bad. At least in the far corner he had some privacy because she never closed her bedroom door when she was entertaining.

* * * *

In the 50's and 60's, teachers didn't have enough knowledge to identify child abuse or learning disabilities. It was common for parents to hit their children as a disciplinary measure. There were no student evaluation groups back then like our present day Child Study Teams. The young boy, however, was blessed with intelligence. So, when he seemed sluggish, his teachers chalked it up to him not having a father and living with a mother that worked long hours. He was what we now call a latchkey kid, a child that goes home after school to an empty house with no supervision.

All his classmates loved Daniel, the quiet kid. Everyone wanted him on their team for group projects. He often considered confiding in a classmate or a teacher but he never did. He could never let on about his mother. He just couldn't lose her. Good or bad, she was all he had. Besides, he genuinely felt he must have been at fault even though he tried so very hard to be a good boy.

His mother, Julie, drove a cab during the day. Being a cabbie turned out to be a pretty good deal for Julie and Daniel. It paid the rent for the tiny apartment which was on the wrong side of town. They got their utilities for free and she was allowed to keep anything after the first

$200.00, which went to the cab's owner. The downside was that she was out of the house for nearly 12 hours a day.

The home, a rundown Victorian, was situated behind railroad tracks. The homeowner, Joe, had inherited the house, a taxi medallion and a cab. Joe always considered himself fortunate to have such generous parents. So, when Julie inquired about renting the attic apartment for herself and her son, he was happy to be financially able to help them out.

Joe would drive his cab all night and made decent money. He was encouraged by friends to get someone to drive days as well. They insisted that it was how he could make real money, by having the cab available 24/7. It was a sweet arrangement for yet another young girl who had both fallen in love and gotten pregnant from one night's act of passion. She swore she had an abortion but family doctors will say that sometimes, one twin can be aborted while the other twin can remain intact and undetected. Until, that is, the mother begins to show. At which point the woman will usually go into a period of denial until it's too late. For that generation, a child would be assigned inappropriate shame and guilt for the crime of being born out of wedlock.

Growing up, Julie had lived with her maternal grandmother after being abandoned by her parents at birth. Grandma was demanding. She never hit her granddaughter but was psychologically cruel, always questioning Julie's decisions. Later in her life it made Julie weak and easy prey for selfish men who would promise her the moon but never deliver. This was all she knew.

* * * *

Daniel planned out his bathroom visits very carefully. His timing was usually fine, however, on one particular night, it definitely was not. On the boy's trip back to the living room the john caught him cowering behind a chair. He said to Julie, "Next time I'll pay double if *he* joins us." Julie was confused. She leaned up on her elbows and focused a sharp glare at her disobedient son. "Get the fuck out," she bellowed to the john. The john got her message loud and clear. He grabbed his clothes and left rather abruptly.

Daniel was stunned. He actually took comfort in the fact that his mother had kicked the guy out and made it clear her son was never going to be part of that business. Julie had been enraged by Daniel and screamed,

"Come here!" The boy obeyed saying, "Mommy, I didn't see anything as I crawled by but I had to go to the bathroom to do number two." Mother interrupted, "You mean to tell me that you didn't even flush – how disgusting! You were instructed to *hold it in* when mommy has company, until the company has left."

* * * *

Julie recalled Senior Day in high school where the senior girls would wait for the younger girls to come into the bathroom. Once inside, they would be surrounded by the seniors and herded into a stall. The toilet had been used by about a dozen seniors and never flushed. It was the *senior surprise*. If you put up a fight, the hazing could be extended for a long time. Julie, a freshman at the time – was petrified. The seniors never really dipped anyone into the bowl. This was more a *fear of the unknown* rather than anything dangerous, but no matter what you called it, it was bullying, pure and simple.

Julie couldn't hold it in, she had to pee. She momentarily forgot about Senior Day and charged into the bathroom. Six seniors pounced. They lifted Julie off her feet and turned her upside down. The seniors moved as a unit pushing into a stall where they began to dip her head into the toilet. They got close, within maybe 10" when they abruptly stopped. One of the senior girls spoke, "You have a choice. We dunk your head all the way in or you voluntarily put your hand in for three seconds." Immediately, Julie reached into the bowl as the upperclassmen counted, "One – two – three!" And it was over. The seniors placed her back on her feet and she was allowed to leave. She didn't even consider washing her hand or gathering her purse and books. The freshman had been assaulted and disgraced so she bolted out of the ladies room, down the corner staircase and out the side door.

She ran home as fast as she could, never looking back and wetting her pants along the way. All the time she was thinking, "I should have held it in…" Her grandmother was surprised to see her granddaughter home so early. Through her tears the young teen told her grandmother her horrible account of what had happened to her in the school bathroom. Her grandmother's only response was, "Oh don't make such a big deal out of nothing." She grabbed Julie's defiled hand and held it under scalding water. She thought the act would purify her granddaughter's hand and also serve as punishment for starting trouble.

* * * *

Julie jumped out of bed totally naked except for her 'come-fuck-me' pumps. The boy hated seeing his mother naked and she smelled terrible. She grabbed him by the neck and dragged him into the bathroom. After one look into the bowl she began to forcibly dip his head in the toilet like a tea bag in a cup of hot water. It was awful. Struggling to breathe and afraid he would die, he dealt with the punishment as best as he could. She looked at her child as a witness to her being caught doing something depraved. She had to reverse the moment by punishing him for offending her. It was already decided that more punishment was still to come.

After shoving his head under the shower, she marched him into the bedroom and yanked him up onto the bed. Unbuckling her shoes, she caught him holding his breath so she said, "O.K. mister perfect, *smell me* – and start with my feet." Her feet were crimped and rancid with pinched toes from wearing cheap shoes two sizes too small. Daniel was nauseous but he didn't dare vomit on his mother's bed. He painfully began to sniff his mother's feet like a puppy dog.

Julie ordered him to start working his way up to her knees then she tugged his hair until he reached her crotch. She held him there for about 10 seconds until she pulled him all the way up to her breast. This was not by accident. She was trying to humiliate her son with incestuous overtures, literally trying to get a rise out of him. Part one of his punishment was to break his spirit. Julie guided the boy's lips directly onto her left nipple. This was pure cruelty. Daniel wasn't buying it but was instead sickened by his mother's actions. She had shamed herself.

Unfortunately for the boy, she took it as yet another rejection which only ratcheted up her anger. As she sat up, she slid her legs over the side of the bed while pulling her son over her knees. The child was terrified. His mother had shown new found strength. He thought his only chance was to submit or die. He chose to submit.

The slaps on his bare bottom were sharp and resonated off the plaster walls and ceilings of the small room. The beating was rhythmic. The boy's penis and testicles were squashed between his mother's thighs, again by design. The pain all the way from backside to his testicles was horrendous.

His mother kept hitting him again and again. The pain was biting but he didn't speak or cry. "Maybe she'll stop soon? Just one or two more?" he prayed. But this time his mother added something new. After many slaps to his buttocks, she spun him over and began to slap his genitalia. It didn't take very long. Within two slaps of incredible pain, he slid off his mother's knees and fell to the floor with a loud thump. As he was falling, in what seemed like slow motion, he looked into his mother's face. He could see his mother's eyes looking up into her head. It was a *crazed* look that frightened him deep inside and scarred him forever.

* * * *

His mother had been abused in the same way, by someone she loved; by someone who was suppose to love her: her grandmother. Julie had been betrayed just as she had betrayed her son. Continuing the multigenerational layers of abuse.

SERGEANT GINA

Reverend Mother Gina Rose Formaggio:

"If you think that becoming a nun is a way to hide from being the absolute best you can be, than you can get out right now. Too many young girls think that this is an easy way for them to slip and slide through life. But that kind of mindset is just an excuse to shirk the responsibilities you owe yourselves."

It's the fall of 2000 and eight young aspirants are about to begin their formal religious education at the Blessed-Sisters' Novitiate. This Formation Program is offered by invitation – only to highly skilled and thoroughly vetted young women. This is their first day of four very difficult years of learning how to become Christian Missionaries. The Blessed-Sisters are also trained to be nurses and teachers. After graduation they are assigned to outposts and catastrophic sites all over the world.

This United States Motherhouse is the second of only two such facilities in existence and is located in New York. The original Motherhouse in Paris is still operating at full capacity. Reverend Mother Gina had trained at the Paris Novitiate. In 1976, at the age of 24, she opened the New York chapter and has presided as its Mother Superior ever since. Today would begin her 7th class.

* * * *

Reverend Mother Gina didn't get the nickname "Sergeant" for nothing. She was as tough as they come, a no nonsense gal. Each one of Gina's classes were drilled again and again: "If you believe that this is a sorority for sheltering women who are afraid to strike out on their own then you're in the wrong place. Don't sell yourselves short. Here, we strive for inner beauty, which makes our outward appearances strong and confident. Here, we learn so we can care for elders, children and the sick. We don't flinch at open sores, terminal diseases or disfigurement. We show respect to all of God's creations and we love our work. We love to serve The Lord."

* * * *

Reverend Mother was born Gina Rose Formaggio in North Bergen, New Jersey, on August 15, 1952. Her two older brothers were highly accomplished members of the Roman Catholic hierarchy. Each brother had been granted the position of Auxiliary Bishop and both worked in the Vatican. Gina had followed their footsteps into religious life. In order to compete with her brothers, she had to study very hard, learning to read and write in Latin while earning a degree in nursing. She also had a background in psychology.

Her brothers, Marco and Luke, were very near in age being born just 11 months apart. They were born in the first post-WWII year, 1946, which began what would become known as the Baby Boomer Generation. Six years older than their sister, the boys were close as brothers but even closer as friends. Early on they had negotiated with their parents and won the right to go through schooling in the same grade and the same class. They made it work by helping and encouraging each other to do their very best. The boys' commitment to learning was incredible and religion was their passion.

Being single-minded about learning led their classmates and friends to think of them as boring. Even their little sister was turned-off to their constant studying. She would playfully taunt her brothers by playing loud rock and roll music and dancing The Twist to their parent's complete delight. Gina nicknamed them Leonardo and da Vinci because they acted like a two dimensional painting that never changed.

When Gina was 4 and the boys were 10, the whole family went to Italy to visit family and friends. In the 1950's the Roman Catholic mass was said in Latin and Ad orientem to the East (where the celebrant faces away from the congregation). It was glorious. The boys were transformed, instantly realizing they wanted to do The Lord's work. Fait accompli. They were struck by the thunderbolt and knew that someday they'd return to Rome forever.

For four years, Marco and Luke were taught by the spirited Jesuits at Xavier High School in New York where they graduated as co-valedictorians. Their undergraduate work began under the tutelage of the Franciscan Friars of the Third Order T.O.R., who founded the Franciscan University of Steubenville in Ohio. In four years, the young men each received two degrees. Marco's degrees were in Psychology and Theology while Luke's were in Philosophy and Theology. The brothers both graduated summa cum laude.

Finally, it was time for the brothers to begin preparing, in earnest, for religious life. For this they chose The Catholic University of America in Washington, D.C. The university was founded in the name of the Roman Catholic Church by Pope Leo XIII and the American Bishops. CUA exists with the approval of the Holy See. In two years they had earned their Masters Degrees in Canon Law.

They stayed three more years and achieved their Doctorates in Canon Law. During the five years they spent in D.C., Marco and Luke had cultivated a wonderful relationship with Cardinal Archbishop R.J. Walsh who ordained the young men and subsequently elevated them to the ranks of Monsignor. The Cardinal then sent them off to Rome and the Papal Offices. The Pope rewarded their scholarship and dedication by assigning them to the prestigious office of The Supreme Tribunal of the Apostalic Signatura. The boys rose rapidly through the ranks and were ultimately consecrated Bishops and later appointed Auxiliaries. Their parents attended the consecrations and were exceedingly proud of their sons.

Gina wasn't able to attend her brothers' ordinations in Washington, D.C. because of her commitment to the Blessed-Sisters' Formation Program in France. At the time, she was only in her third full year and first year of formation. Leaving for any reason was simply not allowed and

Gina feared she would miss their consecrations in Rome as well. However, her superior, Reverend Mother Pia, surprised Gina and her nine classmates by taking them on a pilgrimage to Rome where they actually assisted in Marco and Luke's consecrations.

* * * *

Growing up with two brilliant older brothers had a very positive effect on Gina. It taught her to train herself to listen and retain information while observing body language – especially facial expressions. Her naturally competitive nature made her pay close attention to what her siblings were discussing and she learned how to carefully choose her moments to speak up, making sure her comments were apropos.

Gina's parents were born in Italy – mother Rose in Calabria and father Frank in Naples, both from very religious families. At first they balked at Gina's choice of careers feeling their own devotion to God had pushed her into feeling obligated to choose a life of religious service. Eventually, they came to understand their daughter's true desire to serve The Lord, giving her their full support. They knew that their beautiful Gina Rose, like their sons, had been called to the religious life.

After nine years of attending a Montessori school, Gina was ready to be academically challenged. The Formaggios' obliged their daughter's ambitions by sending her to St. Elizabeth Academy in Convent Station, N.J., where she excelled and began to show signs of brilliance. St. Elizabeth is a prep school and considered amongst the best in the country. And, like her brothers before her, Gina graduated as class valedictorian.

The Blessed-Sisters' Novitiate and its Mother Superior, Elizabeth Pia, called from France and the Formaggio family was thrilled. Incorporated within the Formation Program was attending the Sorbonne University in Paris. It was her #1 choice of colleges.

Growing up, Gina had been influenced by the 1960s where she lived through America's most tumultuous decade. A manufactured war, assassinations, a culture of sex and drugs, The Beatles, women's rights, and most of all, profound change. Unlike her brothers, Gina felt like she needed to experience *many* things in order to be a complete person.

So, she tried marijuana but pot only made her sleepy, silly and overtly irresponsible. Gina dated, however, relationships with men bored her. She thought of them as the guards of her prison cell. A prison cell she felt marriage would have locked her into forever.

She approached adventure the same way, trying to experience everything she could as fast as she could. Nothing satisfied her. By the time Gina was 18 she knew for certain that the challenges she was looking for were waiting for her at the Sorbonne and the Blessed-Sisters' Novitiate in Paris.

The first two years were spent at the Sorbonne completing her Theology and Nursing studies while the following four years were spent at the Formation Program which was very intense and restrictive. After six years of exhaustive training, Gina graduated summa-cum-laude, completed the Blessed-Sisters' Formation Program in outstanding fashion, and had transformed into a spiritually empowered Servant of God.

Gina professed her Final Vows in a small Parisian chapel in a wondrous ceremony celebrated by Cardinal Walsh. He was assisted by Reverend Mother Pia, Marco and Luke and by a slight woman who stood off to the side so as not to be a distraction. Mother Teresa came at the request of her old friend Mother Pia. Gina cried uncontrollably until Mother Teresa hugged her and whispered something very private.

In 1976, 24-year-old Gina Rose Formaggio was given formal orders to start a Blessed-Sisters Program Novitiate in America and act as its Mother Superior. It was the opportunity of a lifetime. Reverend Mother Formaggio packed up her degrees in Theology and Nursing as well as her training skills from Formation and charged off fully armed and ready for the difficult challenges to come.

* * * *

Reverend Mother Gina, *"Hands on ladies. Hands on! This is on the job training. These are things you have to know!"*

After pounding out *who* they were, Reverend Mother would then begin to define *how* her Blessed-Sisters would perform their duties. At any given moment she'd whisper into the ear of one of her charges, "Fall to the floor – bite your tongue – and shake uncontrollably." The other seven would have to react immediately. Gina would closely monitor each and every response. "First and foremost: Identify the symptoms in case the subject is in danger of hurting herself. Simply, find out what's going on!" Then she'd randomly ask, "Sister Pat, what's going on?" Sister Pat started her reply with, "Well…." But Gina cut her off saying, "No, not 'well!' Sister Pat! Please answer my question with expediency, authority and intelligence."

Sister Pat began again, "It appears the patient is having a seizure. The thrashing around could lead to a serious head injury. I'm going to cradle her head for her protection and wait for the danger to run its course." "Excellent!" responded Gina. "Sister Dee, please critique Sister Pat's analysis of the situation." "It was perfect as a preliminary report but the episode will not end there," answered Dee. To which Gina remarked, "Very good Sisters. Very good."

At this point, Gina might whisper new instructions like having the patient respond by vomiting on herself or urinating in the bed. They were hard lessons to learn and never forgotten. There were no exceptions or excuses to taking part in these playacting extremes. Everyone was tested. The only question was: Who's next?

At any given moment the Blessed-Sisters could find themselves at a city morgue, in the workplace of a funeral home, in a hospice treating advanced AIDS patients or at the county examiner's office for an autopsy. As difficult as those jobs were, there was one in particular that stood out as being nearly impossible. Everyone agreed that the Special Needs State Hospital for Children in Rahway, New Jersey was the most unnerving experience of their entire time in training. Profound autism, hydrocephalus, anencephaly, cannibalism and gross deformities were just some of the conditions they encountered at this place of healing. Most of the children here had been abandoned; the truly unwanted. Most of the children lacked the ability to communicate and those few who *could* speak would always ask the same heartbreaking question, "Are you my mommy?"

The Novices had to learn everything, no matter how difficult. It wasn't just learning, it was 360 degrees of a 3-dimensional education. After a week of assisting with the feedings, meds, baths and hugs, the Blessed-Sisters knew their own abilities had been severely tested. The experience explained why Gina was so rigid with her students. She needed to break them down in order to make them stronger. They were the Special Forces of God's Army and there were more challenges to come.

Gina loved serving God and she loved to learn. Mostly, she loved to lead. By becoming a servant of God, she could have all three. Reverend Mother Gina was filled with The Holy Spirit and radiated strength and beauty.

* * * *

The Blessed-Sisters learned discipline. They would wake up at 5:45 a.m. and begin to follow this unyielding schedule:

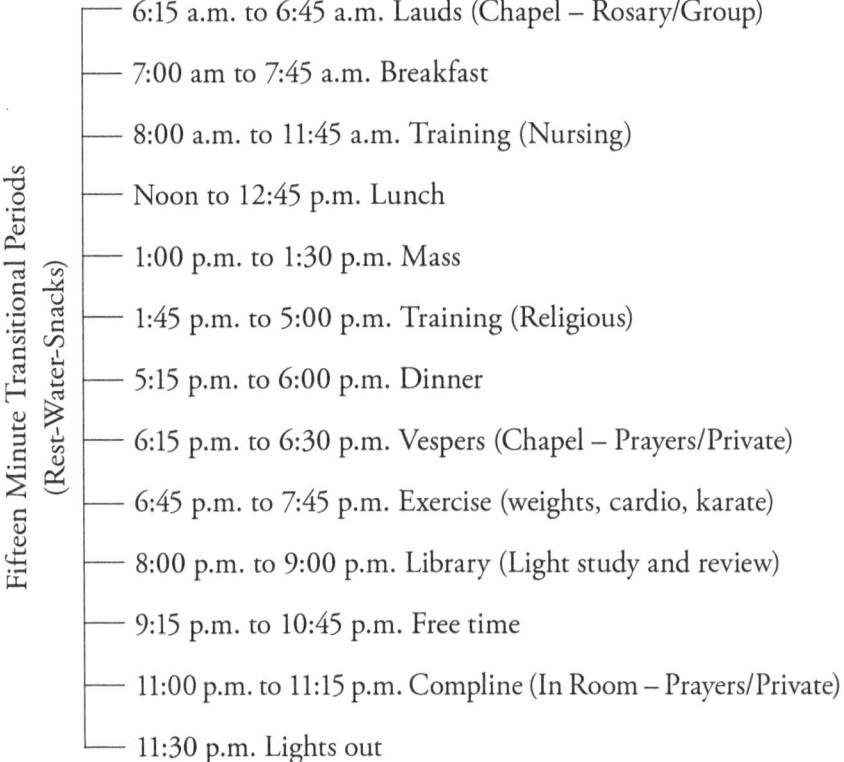

Fifteen Minute Transitional Periods (Rest-Water-Snacks)

- 6:15 a.m. to 6:45 a.m. Lauds (Chapel – Rosary/Group)
- 7:00 am to 7:45 a.m. Breakfast
- 8:00 a.m. to 11:45 a.m. Training (Nursing)
- Noon to 12:45 p.m. Lunch
- 1:00 p.m. to 1:30 p.m. Mass
- 1:45 p.m. to 5:00 p.m. Training (Religious)
- 5:15 p.m. to 6:00 p.m. Dinner
- 6:15 p.m. to 6:30 p.m. Vespers (Chapel – Prayers/Private)
- 6:45 p.m. to 7:45 p.m. Exercise (weights, cardio, karate)
- 8:00 p.m. to 9:00 p.m. Library (Light study and review)
- 9:15 p.m. to 10:45 p.m. Free time
- 11:00 p.m. to 11:15 p.m. Compline (In Room – Prayers/Private)
- 11:30 p.m. Lights out

Reverend Mother Gina and her Blessed-Sisters would repeat this course of action six days a week for four years. Only Sunday's, holidays and emergencies offered a break in the schedule. On those days, family members were allowed short visits. They were also used as travel days.

All of Gina's teaching skills would be greatly challenged in the final year of her second class (1980-1984). That class included Romy Cahill and Mary Ann Santi who were both outstanding Blessed-Sister candidates. For only one year, Gina was blessed with a very special young student who made everyone in the novitiate shake their heads in amazement.

BABY-SISTER

Gina did not record any notes regarding Baby-Sister Kitty during the time Kitty spent with her (Sept. 1983 – Aug. 1984). Reverend Mother would speak about that time from memory and only to her students and religious peers. However, when she did speak Kitty's name she would always shake her head and smile.

These are notes taken from Sister Romy Cahill's journal. The Sisters always had the option to keep journals of their days in training. Romy's notations were stitched into prose in order to have a clearer understanding of the material.

* * *

In September 1983, a 7-year-old "Baby-Sister" Kitty came to stay with Reverend Mother Gina and her second class. Kitty had two beds to choose from. One was with the other girls in the dormitory which had an empty bed next to Sister Romy. The other was a cot-sized trundle bed in Gina's room.

Kitty really didn't sleep; she just rested with her eyes closed. At night she was more inclined to sing beautiful songs or whisper something to someone no one else could see. She might also get up in the middle of the night and quietly tiptoe down to the kitchen for a snack. Of course under Sgt. Gina's rules, other than a visit to the bathroom, the Sisters were not permitted to go anywhere after lights-out.

On one particular night Kitty snuck into the kitchen, dragged over a chair and reached up for the jar of cookies. Behind her two flashlights suddenly lit up and made the kitchen very bright. Without turning around, Kitty softly said, "Wow, I think The Holy Spirit has just arrived." As she turned she saw her Reverend Mother and Sister Romy glaring at her. "Oh no," she said, "I'm in trouble now." Romy walked around the kitchen table and slid Kitty and her chair back over to where it belonged.

Gina quietly answered, "No one is going to be in trouble but if you can keep a secret, how about the three of us girls have two cookies and a half a glass of milk each?" Kitty's eyes lit up, "That's a great plan Mother, but wouldn't three cookies each be more fitting for the occasion?" Gina and Romy were biting their lips trying not to laugh. Reverend Mother had another proposition, "How about I trade you my two cookies for a hug and a kiss?" Kitty smiled. Romy followed suit, "Hey Kit, I'll trade you my stuff for the same agreement?" Kitty replied, "Yes! Those are great deals."

Kitty gave her hugs and kisses and began to eat her bountiful pile of snacks. Romy was on her way back to bed when she heard Kitty engage Gina, "You know Reverend Mother, I could help you sometimes, you know, teach a class? I know the material." Gina nodded saying, "Oh, I bet you could." However, Baby-Sister Kitty had the final say on the subject replying, "And, it would only cost you four cookies and a glass of milk." Gina said, "We'll discuss it tomorrow but now it's time to get back into bed. Are you coming with me or going back with the girls?" Prophetically Kitty said, "I'm going with you Reverend Mother" and continued to chatter away. The two walked toward Reverend Mother's room with Gina holding Kitty's left hand while Kitty held her Mary Magdalene doll in the other. Romy finally went to bed having heard enough and shaking her head in total amazement.

* * * *

One night, Kitty was lying in her bed when she suddenly asked, "Romy, why do humans make fun of angels?" Romy asked, "What do you mean, Kit?" Kitty explained, "Movies always show angels like they're dopey humans who lead boring lives." Romy held Kitty's hand and said, "Those aren't proper depictions are they?" "No," said Kitty. "In Heaven, we sometimes watch human movies. This one picture shows angels begging to become humans so they can have fun." Kitty was referring to the German film 'Wings of Desire' which Romy had no reference to because it wasn't released until three years later. "Or that other one where some older man says, 'Every time you hear a bell ring another angel gets his wings.' How silly, angels don't even have wings."

Kitty sat up to continue, "In Heaven, there is no time and space goes on forever. There is no need for air or gravity because we don't breathe and we naturally move in all directions. But the best thing about Heaven is that there is no fighting, no wars and no sadness. Everything is peaceful. It lets us sing, dance and honor Our Maker."

Romy was fixed in rapt attention to Kitty's every word. "There was evil in Heaven, just once, but Michael – he's an archangel – kicked the bad guy right out of Heaven. The Lord actually cried because one of His children had betrayed Him.

"Romy, angels are God's creations and the only reason we're here is to serve The Lord.

"Anyway, all humans are little pieces of God the Father. When they get to heaven, those little pieces are put back together and become a part of our Lord. There are still a few humans in Heaven like John the Apostle and Mary Magdalene. And some say the Blessed Mother is also there but no one has seen her since she arrived nearly 2000 years ago."

* * * *

Kitty was watching, along with the other Sisters, a film lesson on planets, galaxies and the universe. After about a half hour she spoke up which shocked Reverend Mother and the girls. She wondered why people would take more than a 'cursory' look at the stars. *She* knew the stars held no answers. "You guys really don't understand the bigness of space. I guess it's just too hard to imagine.

"Your galaxy, the 'Milky Way,' has 200 billion stars. Your neighboring galaxy, 'Andromeda,' also has 200 billion stars. Both galaxies are drifting toward each other. In a mere 5 billion years those two galaxies will violently merge. So, question: How many of the stars will actually collide?"

Not one of the Blessed-Sisters even attempted a guess. Gina just smiled. Kitty announced, "NONE! The stars are just too far apart. However, giant gas clouds and space dust – which exist between the stars – will ignite from friction and cause a fireworks type of explosion forging those galaxies into something new and spectacular.

"Reverend Mother, if you took a grain of sand and cut it in half and cut it in half and cut it in half, again and again, a trillion times, that super-mini-microscopic piece of sand is the total amount of energy that The Lord uses to power all the planets, stars and galaxies in the entire universe. And there are *billions* of galaxies throughout the universe. The rest of God's Power resides in Heaven. Anyway...."

The Blessed-Sisters and Gina just sat there feeling very small. Humbled. Kitty ran off to the kitchen for her four cookies and a glass of milk.

On another evening, Kitty's head was tilted while she was intently listening to someone or something. It was just like those three children at Fatima, who claimed they had been speaking with the Blessed Mother. Here too it was made very clear that no one was allowed to take part in or interfere in any way. Sister Romy instinctively knew the meeting was very private so she turned and began to drift off to sleep. However, she did overhear Kitty say, "It's so silly isn't it?"

Re: Baby-Sister Kitty – Journal entries by Sister Romy Cahill 9/1/83 – 8/31/84.

* * * *

A few days later, Baby-Sister reluctantly accompanied Sister Gina and Reverend Mother Pia to the home of John and Carol McGuire of Plains, New Jersey. Two weeks later, the McGuire's formally adopted Kitty. She lived in Plains for 10 years completing her primary and secondary educations. After high school graduation, she entered the Blessed-Sisters' Formation Program in Paris at the age of 17.

BLESSED-SISTERS IN TRAINING

The following notations were taken directly from Reverend Mother's daily journals and reworked into vignettes so they would be more easily understood. Like everything she did, her contemporaneous notes made for an abundance of memory squares of humanness, woven together into a patchwork quilt of her life.

* * * *

At lunch one afternoon the Sisters were served soda, ice cold water, sweet fruit juices and hot tea with honey. "Drink up ladies but when you're finished don't go to the bathroom." As they finished lunch, they all became quiet wondering, "What now?" They knew the party was over when Reverend Mother led them into the bathroom. Once inside, Gina handed them large plastic cups with their names on them. "OK girls, fill 'er up!" The Sisters were standing in a circle, slightly embarrassed, but entered the stalls one by one to oblige their Reverend Mother.

Sister Bernie placed her cup on the round work table then knelt down to tie her shoe. Sister Sarah had just placed her cup down and was standing very uncomfortably awaiting further instructions.

Bernie inadvertently wound up behind Sarah when, quite accidentally, Sarah passed wind very close to Bernie's face. Bernie jerked her head to the side and shot Sarah a dirty look. Whispering aloud Bernie said, "Asshole!" Reverend Mother put her chin on Bernie's shoulder and whispered, "Please kiss the 'asshole' and tell her your sorry. "Gina disliked when her

Blessed-Sisters broke decorum. She wanted to convey that: words spoken in anger were a obvious sign of weakness.

A very confused Sister Bernie leaned over to kiss Sarah on the buttocks when Reverend Mother pulled her back by the collar and said, "Kiss her on the cheek, the one by her ear and whisper 'I'm sorry,' and mean it." Bernie respectfully complied.

The wicker work table in the bathroom held place cards with each Blessed-Sister's name on it. The Sisters were ordered to match their cups with their place card. After finishing Gina said, "When you're done, stand around the table in front of your cups.

"Ladies, years ago, there were no tests for diabetes. So, doctors would taste the urine of a patient to check for its sweetness. That's what we are doing today. Start by taking your cup in hand and gently wipe the rim, removing any foreign particles. Now put your cups down and everyone take one step to the right. That's whose urine you're going to taste. Besides testing for sugar, I want you to observe for density (fiber), color (darker urine indicates dehydration) and odor (sweet/salty/sour) and blood.

"Grab your neighbor's cup girls and taste, and *only* taste, for information. DO NOT SWALLOW!" Slowly, all eight Sisters took hold of their neighbor's cup, closed their eyes, tilted their cups up to their mouths, and inserted their tongues. The Sisters were not feeling well as they put their cups down but they knew vomiting meant they'd all have to repeat the exercise again. So, a very queasy bunch of Sisters began to note their findings.

* * * *

At two months into her on-the-job training, Sister Sarah was distressed. She had always been regimented, easily able to follow orders but now the aspirant couldn't concentrate on performing her duties.

One night, she became physically ill with nausea, diarrhea and cramps. The Sister crept out of bed and ran across the hallway to the lavatory. She went into the first stall and bolted the door behind her. Sitting on the bowl, she wrapped her arms around her waist and doubled over in excruciating pain. Sarah pushed and pushed, trying to relieve gas or force a bowel movement. To her utter shock and horror, she felt something begin to slip out of her vagina. Reaching down between her legs, she pulled out a slippery thumb-sized object. The stall areas were dimly lit – it was a no reading thing. So she gently lifted the object up to her eyes for a better look. Though foreign to her, it was unmistakable. The little alien had eyes and two arms fused to its main body. It was a miscarriage. Shock rapidly turned to grief and Sarah wept.

    Suddenly, a broom stick came over the top of the stall door. The stick was being held by a hand which was reaching down tapping the door lock open. After two tries the door swung open. Standing in the doorway was Reverend Mother Gina. With both hands she pulled Sarah's head against her bosom. Sarah was relieved to have her Reverend Mother with her. "Reverend Mother, I need to show you something," Sarah whispered through a stream of tears. The Sister held up the remains of the fetus and asked, "Should she be baptized?" Gina answered, "Yes and since a baptism can be performed by anyone in an emergency situation, why don't you baptize your little angel?" Sarah was relieved to hear such a wonderful idea. Reverend Mother pulled out her plastic bottle of Holy Water and gave it to her student. Sarah recited, "I baptize you in the name of the Father and of the Son and of the Holy Spirit, amen."

    Sarah hugged her Reverend Mother who took the remains and placed the unborn fetus into a plastic baggie for proper disposal. Nothing was said about her having been pregnant; it wasn't necessary. Sarah didn't need to hear it. She was a brilliant Sister candidate with a bright future. But Sarah did have a question. "Mother, how did you know?" Gina answered, "Women display poor ability to control bodily functions when they're pregnant, like holding gas." Reverend Mother was referring to her incident with Sister Bernie. Due to hormonal changes a woman with child can also be forgetful, very irritable and short on patience.

    Reverend Mother helped Sarah to stand. She hugged Gina and thanked her for being there. A grief stricken Sarah washed herself and, totally drained both mentally and physically, went to bed and fell asleep almost instantly.

* * * *

Just like the Marines, Navy Seals and Army Rangers, Gina and her Blessed-Sisters had their own secret salutes and rituals. When passing their Reverend Mother in the hallway, they would whisper "Morning Mother" or simply, they could be silent and bend their right arm at the elbow – raising their hand up to their shoulder. Each of their right hands would have the middle finger crossed over their index finger with the thumb curled upward.

The crossed fingers was the sign for "truth" and the upward curled thumb was the sign for "justice." Together it was meant as a reference to God's Truth and Justice. In either case Reverend Mother's reply would be a very serious, single wide-eyed nod.

* * * *

At least one day a month, Reverend Mother would assemble her eight Sisters in an empty work room. With these young nuns totally unclothed, they clutched a crucifix and rosary beads in one hand and a Bible in the other. Forming a square two to a side, with Reverend Mother in the middle, they would walk the square's perimeter counter-clockwise, at a slow knee-high pace. Their arms were bent at the elbow. Their arms and legs swung in opposite directions to one another. Left knee up, right elbow down. Right knee up, left elbow down.

This wasn't an exercise in human sexuality. Instead, it was their Reverend Mother rewiring the way her students thought by making them face their own humanity and their own human needs and weaknesses. She needed to break them of worldly inhibitions, attitudes and prejudices. This is how they would learn. It was a template for selflessness and a blueprint for caregivers. This was the discipline.

While they marched they chanted this mantra:

> *"This was His Promise*
> *He is the Truth*
> *This was His Justice*
> *He is the Proof"*

* * * *

Early in their third year, Sister Gina would mark the time with a frightening challenge. "More than halfway home children and I've got something I want you to seriously consider. I'm sure you've all heard of the term 'self-flagellation.' You may have even read about it in the novel *The Da Vinci Code* or have seen it performed in the film *The Black Robe*.

"This very coarse and heavily woven rope, complete with tight knots, barbs and beads is called a flagellator. Those of you who plan on staying for two more years of training will need to flog themselves just once, on their bare backs, as proof of their love for and commitment to Our Lord. This is the discipline for those who serve."

The Sisters were silent as they awaited further instruction. The rope looked menacing and its strands had actually irritated their palms after they were ordered to feel and examine its tentacles. The Sisters were told to go into the locker room to remove their blouses, jumpers, shoes and socks. Then they were to return to the instructional room with a dry bath towel covering their frontal area, knees to chin. After each Sister carried out their orders, their neighbor to the right would clean their wounds with Betadine and Neosporin.

When no one volunteered to go first, 50-year-old Reverend Mother removed her blouse and bra, walked to the middle of the room and flogged her bare back with a snap of the flagellator. The Sisters winced at the slap of the cords tearing into her skin. The act left a bloody imprint from the top of her left shoulder down and moving outward in a fan-like shape which ended just above her waist. Upon closer inspection, the Sisters could see the scarring of at least six other times she had flogged herself. The scars were in varying degrees of color, the older ones were lighter while the more recent were darker. Over the years, time had beautifully blended the colors on her skin. It looked like an elaborate, artful tattoo.

Almost robotically, Reverend Mother walked back to her place while handing the rope to Sister T.C. The young trainee tried not to think about it; it was just too scary to contemplate. Dutifully, she walked to the middle of the classroom, dropped her towel and took the weapon to her back. She felt a rush of stinging pain but she picked up her towel and returned to her place handing the rope to Sister Bernie.

One by one all the Sisters carried out their requirement. They all moved around the work table where the medications and cotton balls were waiting. No further words were spoken except for Reverend Mother who said, "If you want to eat dinner, Ms. Elsa has prepared a light meal for you. However, no further responsibilities are required for this evening. The self-flagellation exercise is to bring you closer to God. To complete the process, meditation and quiet contemplation is recommended which you may do on your own. Either way, I will see you all in the morning at 11:00, which is about four hours later than usual. And ladies, I'm extremely proud of you. This is a very special group. Thank you." With that, all eight went straight to their beds all lying face down with their backs bared, very sore and again questioning their courage to go on. The day had been too stressful. They had no appetite or the strength to do anything else.

At about 7:00 a.m. Gina went to each of her charges with Neosporin and Motrin. She wanted to make sure the wounds were dry and scabbing after 14 hours. She spent some time with each, whispering something so only she and that student knew what was said. When rounds were completed her Sisters were filled with the Holy Spirit and joyously contemplating what they had accomplished in the name of the Lord. Gina remembered what Reverend Mother Pia had told her when she was a student. "You can always get the attention of The Lord when you suffer in His name. True suffering is good for the soul." Gina let them sleep in. It had been a brutal exercise and they needed their rest and time to heal.

At 11:00 a.m., Reverend Mother's assistant, Sister Romy Cahill from Ireland, went into the dormitory to rouse the Sisters and redress their wounds. They had been sleeping since Reverend Mother Gina had left them. She had a message for them that Reverend Mother would not be joining them because her wounds appeared to be infected.

The news startled the Sisters as they always thought their Reverend Mother was invincible. Fortunately, Sister Romy was one of Reverend Mother's former students from her 2nd class and she had two circular scars on her left hand just above the thumb and six scarred lines on her back to prove it. She was a fantastic nurse who excelled in emergency room medicine. Leading by example, Romy almost never spoke. She was always around but never prominently there. The Sisters were surprised when she spoke that afternoon. They all thought that Romy was probably being groomed to someday take over as Mother Superior when Reverend Mother retired.

They were shocked when she said they could briefly visit with their Reverend Mother in her bedroom, a place they were never invited into before. As Sister Romy opened the door they could see the room was very sparse with only a bed, rocking chair, closet and a bureau with a mirror. On the mirror were four photographs. There was one of her parents and brothers at home in N.J.; one of Gina at 14 with Cardinal Wojtyla at the Vatican; one of Gina, Reverend Mother Pia, Antonia Spingola and Kitty at Kitty and Tonia's 8th grade graduation; and one of Gina, Reverend Mother Pia and Mother Teresa in France, 1976. The afghan on her bed and the shawl on the back of her chair were both made by her mother.

As they crept further into her room they found their Reverend Mother curled up in her rocking chair reading 'Life of Christ' by Bishop Fulton J. Sheen. Gina was surprised to see all eight of her charges quietly walk into her room. "What's this? I'm not dead. Sister Romy's nursing skills are spectacular so I'm on the mend. I'm going to take one more day of rest while Sister Romy instructs you for the next 12 hours on symptom recognition and immediate evaluation. It's a triage class and she's the best. Sister has recently been stationed in Iraq and Afghanistan so keep your minds in sponge-mode and absorb."

After a few minutes, Sister Bernie asked her Reverend Mother if they could examine *her* wounds. Again, to their complete surprise, Gina stood up, removed her shawl and her white "Even Jesus had a Mother" T-shirt, once again baring her breasts as she lay face down on her bed. For the next 15 minutes they gave opinions, shared observations and asked questions of Sister Romy to the satisfaction of Reverend Mother who remained quiet, acting out the part of a wounded patient. The Sisters were very involved and Romy's explanations were precise and thorough. It was quite a learning experience.

Before the Sisters left the room, they passed by Reverend Mother's bed and individually whispered, "Truth and Justice" to Gina's profound happiness.

* * * *

The young ladies had trained for drawing blood. In fact, they had already received certificates as legally registered phlebotomists. Gina wanted them to draw blood from each other as this was an exercise in consideration.

Drawing blood while having your blood drawn makes you want to carry out your assignment as professionally and painlessly as possible.

* * * *

The Sisters dreaded the start of each morning. They never knew what was coming next. Gina walked into the science lab and announced, "Leeches! Yes ladies, it's 'Leech Day.'" This was purely old school but very effective. The health benefit provided by these little creatures hides in their saliva which prevents blood from clotting. That allows oxygenated blood to continuously flow through a wounded area until the veins repair, and regain circulation.

Gina had already wheeled in a large bell jar of leeches. "Girls, I want you to observe and feel the value of what these little creatures of God can do to help humans." It was another rough day. As they went off to bed, Sister reminded them that, in the wilderness or in extreme situations, you have to be resourceful and use every patch and stitch available.

The most terrifying morning orders came on the day that Reverend Mother wheeled a large covered wicker basket into the lab. "Watch closely Sisters." Gina stuck her left hand under the cloth cover. They could see her moving her hand like she was stirring a pot of spaghetti. After a few moments they heard a noise, a snap, then there was a violent shaking under the cloth cover. Gina winced and quickly pulled out her hand. It was bleeding from two little round holes just above her thumb. The Sisters could see the scars from maybe another dozen older holes in that same area on her hand.

"Sisters, this is a snake bite. Allow it to bleed because we don't always know if it's poisonous so we have to assume it is. So, question, 'How do you get the poison out?'" A tense silence filled the room until one Sister nervously answered, "Suck it out, Mother?" "Yes! Brave lady, Sister Bernie. Correct, but with an explanation. Modern science now tells us that the poison you suck out can go right to your brain through a cavity in a tooth. Also, a person may have the HIV virus so, now-a-days, we carry certain 21st century tools with us at all times. Like this aspirator that is good for squeezing fluids in or for drawing poisons out.

Before getting bitten Reverend Mother allowed them a 15 minute recess to gather themselves. After their break they lined up, each taking their turn by placing their hands in the basket. Then they'd run over to the table waiting for the others to be baptized by blood.

The circular fang holes would also become permanent scars, affectionately referred to as "Sarge's Gemini." All 60 of Gina's students proudly bear the honor of the experience.

* * *

From time to time Reverend Mother would regale her students with stories about her older students.

"In my second class there was a Sister named Mary who came to me with a background in Zoology and a complete understanding of animal reproduction. She had been introduced to the Blessed-Sisters' Formation Program because she had been sent to a nunnery at age 14 when it was discovered that she was pregnant. She was rebellious and quite a challenge to yours truly. It seems the girl was promised, by a 17 year old boy that, if she had sex with him, he would pull out long before he came inside her. This was all the assurance she needed, deferring to the wisdom of a much 'older' and 'wiser' schoolmate who had the added irresistible charm of being her high school's star quarterback and most popular player.

"Mary loved sending shockwaves through the convent and delighted in revealing that several weeks before her prom night rendezvous, she took a carrot – stuck the fat end into a jar of Vaseline – and inserted it into her vaginal opening so she could tear her hymen. She was literally trying to break her own cherry so it wouldn't hurt during intercourse with the quarterback and to make it seem like she had done it before. On prom night, everything went off without a hitch. The real deed was now done.

"I told Mary that while she did have a vast knowledge of the reproduction systems for almost every known animal, she knew very little about the most important reproduction system: human reproduction. Mary still didn't understand how she got pregnant. 'After all, he did pull out.'" The Sisters were captivated by Reverend Mother's story, hanging on every word.

"Sister Fran, why did Sister Mary get pregnant?" Sister Fran jumped up for her answer, "The reason is obvious Reverend Mother, never trust the word of a guy!" To which, again, everyone laughed. "Sorry Mother," said Fran. "But the actual answer does lie in the male side of human sexuality." "Very good," Reverend Mother was intrigued. "Please continue Sister." Fran took a deep breath and began her explanation, "After a man achieves an erection, prostate fluid lubricates the urinary tract to make it easier for sperm to travel through. The culprit here is that a small amount of sperm sneaks out of the scrotum, through the vas deferens, and goes up, into the prostate. At the start of intercourse, there already is sperm being squeezed out of the penis and into the vagina long before a man reaches orgasm. That's why pulling out is not at all reliable when used as a method of birth control."

"Fantastic – spot on!" crowed Reverend Mother. The seven other Sisters stood and applauded their classmate for her riveting and accurate explanation.

* * * *

The Sisters were very curious; they wanted to know more about Sister Mary. They begged for another story.

Reverend Mother proposed a different question: "A man found a bat flying around the light in his attic. He instinctively grabbed an old beach towel and snapped at the bat, mid-flight. The bat dropped to the floor stunned and squealing. With a wooden paint stick, the man pinned the bat's head and teeth while picking up the bat by pinching the wings behind the animal's back. However, by morning the man had developed a very high temperature and was sweating profusely. He went to the Emergency Room where he was diagnosed with rabies.

"The man swore he wasn't bitten and an examination of his hands showed nothing, not even a scratch. So ladies, how did he catch rabies?"

Seeing the fully attentive but bewildered looks on the faces of her troops, Reverend Mother answered the question herself. "Sister Mary knew that you get rabies from a bat's saliva; you don't have to be bitten. She knew that rabies is a virus. It's a virus we get from bats because bats are carriers and they are rarely infected by the virus. Rats can give you rabies as well as dogs and other hairy animals that, in turn, get rabies from infected fleas and other mammals. Mary knew that the infected saliva gets absorbed right through human skin and into the bloodstream. It isn't necessary to be bitten to contract rabies."

"I know, I know … bats and rabies as a story isn't much fun but it's interesting to me. Anyway, I'll tell you girls something that I promise will capture your attention."

The girls all leaned in toward their Reverend Mother. Reverend Mother started off with an unofficial nursing rule, "Nurses, especially Sister/Nurses can be catty, shameless scamps. (Giggles). They cannot keep secrets and they love telling embellished stories and can be such troublemakers that surely perdition awaits them." As she spoke, Gina would continuously scan the faces of her young nuns, looking for signs and confirmation of her message. The Sisters leaned in further, widened their eyes and held their collective breaths. This was going to be good.

Reverend Mother continued. "A man in his mid-seventies had been admitted to the hospital the night before. He was a smallish black man who had complained of chest pain and dizziness. So, there he was in the ICU with all sorts of tubes in him and many lines coming out of his arms and chest, all of which were attached to electronic monitors.

"His wife, an attractive woman also in her mid-seventies, sat beside him. They had no children or other family members. It was just the two of them looking into each other's eyes but not a word was spoken. In fact the only sounds in the room were the bells, whistles and clicks that came from the machines to which he was attached. Word of this unique gentleman had begun to circulate throughout the hospital. Everyone seemed to know his not-so-secret secret.

"Nurses, both regular and clerical, kept running lists of things you would see in a hospital. Worst deformity, most obese, biggest GORK (which is nurse-speak for GOD ONLY REALLY KNOWS why they're alive), etc. However, the absolutely most popular list was the one for penis size, non-erect.

"The patient had already taken a battery of tests and was awaiting the preliminary results. The ICU night nurses who had prepped the gentleman were amazed when they removed his clothing. Considering most experienced nurses have seen every type of human in all shapes and sizes, it was a giant surprise when they saw his penis. One older nurse began to palpitate and had to run out of the room to catch her breath. It reminded the others of that boastful nurse who had to run away after seeing the Elephant Man. The long and short of it was that it was about the size of a 20 oz. plastic soda bottle. It just didn't seem like the appropriate appendage for that particular body. The voyeur parade of nurses, orderlies and techs had begun. Guys, girls, security guards and even the hospital chaplain, all came in to take a peek. However, the ICU nurses had gone too far. While the patient genuinely liked the attention, his wife whispered to the head nurse, 'They can look but they can't touch. That's my husband!'"

* * * *

Banter like this would go on into the wee hours at the convent. Reverend Mother prayed for sponge like brains in her students that would absorb the continuous flow of information. Computers never shut down and neither did the minds of the Blessed-Sisters.

When Gina was in the last year of her Blessed-Sisters' Formation Program in Paris, she was ordered to do her internship at La Clinique pour Femmes in Provence. Her assignment was to run the nurses' section of the hospital.

Gina was in her office when she overheard a conversation between two of her Information Desk assistants, Mary and an older nun named Sister Margaret. The young assistant was on the phone with an irate woman who was calling about a child that died at the hospital during delivery about 40 years ago.

The young assistant was being advised by the older nun to ward off the woman who was, "Just looking for someone to sue." Sister Margaret was retired but volunteered her time helping out the younger Sisters and standing as a guardian of the hospital. Many years before she had been a sister/student there and had worked her way up to Nursing Director. She also helped raise donations for the hospital's many improvements and expansions over the years. Sr. Margaret's final instruction to Mary was, "Tell her to stay away from the hospital."

Sister Gina called Mary into her office. She then asked her for all the facts regarding the prior phone call with the irate woman. Mary explained how the woman wanted information about the delivery room that day, 40 years ago, because she felt that her just born brother had been carelessly dropped. The woman believed the newborn was dropped by the delivery doctor or an assisting nurse. Sister Margaret had advised her that the woman was "…just looking to sue us - the hospital - so we shouldn't give her any information."

Several days later, Gina called Mary and Sister Margaret to her office. They found that the irate woman, Ms. Beatrice Kane, was also sitting in her office. Gina wanted the woman to know exactly what happened that morning 40 years before. She also wanted Mary and, especially Sister Margaret, to observe how a Catholic hospital resolves issues.

A couple of minutes later an even older nun, Sister Regina Anthony, walked into the room. She was frail, using a walker, and was limping badly. Sister Regina sat down with help from the others and began to explain what happened in the delivery room on that fateful morning. It was revealed that Ms. Kane's mother delivered a stillborn. The elder Sister continued explaining that Ms. Kane's mother, Ms. Jane Larkin, began to bleed-out and the doctor called for all hands to help stop the bleeding. After Ms. Larkin was stabilized, Sister Regina said she went back to the dressing table to take the stillborn up to the hospital morgue. Sister said that as she picked up the child from the table she slipped on the blood soaked floor. But, rather than dropping the child to free her hands to grab the table, she fell awkwardly on her hip and broke it in two places. "I held the child tightly to my breast. It would have been disrespectful to let him fall. Even in death the child was beautiful, a beautiful little boy and a child of God.

"The complications from the fall have been with me ever since." Sister made it very clear that she had no regrets and that she would do it again – not letting a stillborn drop to the floor.

Sister Gina said, "Thank you Sister Regina. Your continued devotion to Our Lord is an inspiration to us all." With that, Sister Regina left the room but not before Ms. Kane gave her a hug. Ms. Kane then thanked Gina and left with happy tears of relief. Gina didn't dismiss Mary and Sister Margaret. "Why would we want to keep something a secret?" Sister Gina was angry. "If people can't get truthful answers from us then who can they get them from? If we don't live by the rules we espouse then what the hell are we doing here?"

Reverend Mother took a deep breath and said, "The Bible is very clear on this issue." Matthew 4:16 And the Lord said, "Woe to you Scribes and Pharisees who preach the letter of the law but don't keep it."

"Mary, if you have a question on anything, ask *me*! Don't ever advise anyone to *stay away* from the hospital. If the hospital gets sued, so be it. If someone alleges a mistake we will then investigate. We must always be searching for the truth. Young Sister candidates should be able to decipher good advice from bad.

"Truth and Justice is the code we live by. We must always stay above reproach. We work for God. If the archbishop has a problem with that, then have him call *me* from his palatial chancery office in Paris."

Gina dismissed Mary and Sister Margaret, giving the older nun the 'you should have known better' stare as Margaret walked out, with the rope that holds the 8" crucifix around her waist, twisted in a knot.

"The moral of the story is: Stay focused. Always remember our primary objective is to serve. By the way, Mary is the same young lady from my second class that you know now as Sister Mary."

* * * *

Rev. Mother Gina speaking to her students:

"Blessed-Sister, Mary Ann Santi, had her baby and gave her up for adoption to a wonderful young couple from New Jersey. At the age of 15, her family sent her to the Blessed-Sisters' Novitiate to live under the care and supervision of Reverend Mother Pia.

"Mary wasn't a 'bad-girl,' in fact, she was brilliant and unabashed. She became a valued member of the novitiate by, counseling teenage women about human sexuality.

"In my last year of formation I was assigned as the nursing director at the Women's Clinic in Provence. I asked Mother Pia if I could take Mary with me as an assistant. Pia thought it was a great idea.

"After taking Final Vows in 1976, I was assigned to start a 2nd Blessed-Sisters' Novitiate in New York City. Mary Ann was about to start four years at the Sorbonne. I told her that if she accomplished all her college goals she would be welcomed to begin her Formation Program with my 2nd class 1980-84.

"She graduated from college with honors and arrived in America in August 1980 to begin Formation. During her four years here she bonded with all nine Blessed-Sisters especially Romy Cahill. She wrote and published articles about teen topics. And even welcomed a special meeting with her 7 year old daughter.

"After finishing Formation, Mother Pia called Mary and told her the Vatican was interested in a Blessed-Sister to assist in the Papal Office. I don't know much about her duties in Rome but she sent me a letter saying: 'The Pope said to say hello.'

"Not bad for a woman who was unfairly judged, for her entire life, by one indiscretion."

* * * *

Reverend Mother Gina Rose Formaggio:

"Our patients' care and consideration is paramount. They are our objective."

"Once, while working in a hospice with Reverend Mother Pia, I was washing the hair of a tiny 97-year-old woman. I was doing so on my lunch break because she knew her time was near and she wanted everything to be perfect. Her one request was that her hair be washed and set so she would be ready to meet her Maker. I was on cloud nine just being so close to someone who was about to be taken by the Lord and welcomed the moment as a new beginning. She had had a long and wonderful life.

"All of a sudden the door swung open and a male nurse, a narcissistic idiot, said, 'Hey Gina, why [are] you wastin' [your] time with her, she'll be dead before your shift is over.' I immediately shot him a dirty look so he closed the door and left. When I turned back toward the old woman she was staring at me with a quizzical expression on her face. She asked, 'I wonder how he knew?' Then she drifted off into a peaceful and everlasting sleep.

"Anger filled my body. I jumped up and stormed into the lunchroom down the hall where I lit into that jackass with both barrels, ending with a solid right to his mouth. Spare the rod; spoil the idiot."

* * * *

One of the most legendary stories that helped define Reverend Mother Gina's reputation occurred in the mid-sixties when she was about 14 years old.

She was on an Italian summer vacation with her parents. Her parents went ahead to see family and friends in Naples and Calabria, while Gina stayed in Rome under the watchful eyes of her brothers. Being the sister of two college students doing their internships in the Vatican afforded her some very special privileges. She was allowed to study and research in the Vatican Library where she was surrounded by many members of the clergy from all over the world. Those around her were researching various assignments and were simply brilliant.

One day, she found herself in a heated discussion with a Polish archbishop named Karol Jozef Wojtyla. The archbishop was researching a project for then Pope Paul VI. Its subject matter was in reference to human sexuality.

The archbishop was amazed that young Gina spoke Latin fluently and even sprinkled in a few Polish phrases. He welcomed the opinions of the female student and took her into his confidence on highly intimate aspects of his research. To his profound surprise, she was both intelligent and straightforward with her responses.

Gina was outraged by the archbishop's belief that coitus interruptus was wrong because it wouldn't be fair to the woman. She continued that penile withdrawal, just before ejaculation, would not guarantee that a woman wouldn't become pregnant nor would the act mean it would necessarily be unfair to a woman's enjoyment. Gina ended her argument by saying all animal species enjoy the heavenly reward for the act of reproduction. In her private thoughts the young student wondered if the archbishop had any personal experience to support his position.

The archbishop countered with sexual relations having a natural order designed by God. This natural order could never allow for withdrawal, alternative positions, abortion, or homosexuality. Needless to say the discussion went on for hours with a large number of the clergy scholars taking part. One of Gina's brothers had come to take her to dinner and was amazed at his little sister holding court with such a knowledgeable collection of men.

Pope Paul VI eventually agreed with the archbishop (who would become the third longest reigning and amongst the most conservative Popes in History.) The encyclical would become known as Humane Vitae (of human life), much to the applause of some and to the great disappointment of others. Years later, Pope John Paul II would unexpectedly cross paths with the angry young student several years after taking her vows. The Pope, who would be nominated for sainthood, looked into her eyes with his approval as if to say, "Thank God – now we're on the same team."

Eighteen years later, the Pope's angry young pupil would design an alternative way for gay men to safely engage in sexual intercourse with other men. Gina had worked the front lines with her Blessed-Sisters fighting the AIDS epidemic of the eighties. She washed the open sores of the men with the devastating virus. The pain, the continuous suffering, the hospital costs and heartbreaking disfigurement all added up to being a grossly unfair price to pay for having physical contact with a loved one. Gina discovered early on that homosexuality is bestowed from birth and not a lifestyle choice or an abomination as the church still preaches.

After watching so many suffer from AIDS, Gina was compelled to come up with something – anything – to eradicate this virus. The most talented doctors in the world were also scrambling for a cure and none had been successful. Then it came to her. If she couldn't help cure it, maybe she could prevent it! After years of tinkering, she invented something that would ultimately be a wonderful, life-saving breakthrough for the male members of the gay community. She painstakingly wrote out a blueprint for a medical operation that would give men the permanent protection they needed. If successful, she would then be able to alter it to help the women.

Using every resource she had, Gina contacted hospitals and surgeons all over the world, explaining her idea and sending out a detailed synopsis of her proposed procedure. One by one, each had politely declined but wished her well. They just didn't think it would work. In a desperate hour, Sister had received some great news. A plastic surgeon had heard about the nun's project and offered to organize a research team that would be supported by two million dollars in donations. The doctor himself was a gay man who was fascinated by Gina's bold ideas. He told Sister that the money was donated by several American citizens. They too were impressed by Sister's genuine concern for the welfare of others. The surgeon promised to keep his fingers crossed and his thumb curled upward.

* * * *

The Sisters had had a particularly rough day. Reverend Mother Gina was in the final days of this groups' fourth year of on-the-job training. Gina was standing just outside the locker area of their barracks-type dormitory. "Oh, she's still a bitch!" said Sister Bernie. "Why don't I just leave now; she hates me," said Sister T.C. Everything hurt. Their toes, feet, ankles, calves, backs, necks – *everything*. The Sisters were in dire need of showers, food and sleep. They were battered and bruised, weary as coalminers after a twelve hour shift. So when their Reverend Mother silently opened the door, they figured they were all doomed. Almost four years of training gone to waste.

To the absolute astonishment of all the Blessed-Sisters, Reverend Mother started to cry. She had never shown them any sign of emotional weakness before. "You will be leaving for your homes in two days and you may not come back. I wanted to make sure my message is getting through, that Jesus is real. He is the absolute truth. That the further away from sin you get, the closer you are to the purest understanding of Our Lord and His Grace. Even if you don't partake in the sin, just being near it becomes a distraction from the truth. It inhibits your ability to be complete."

Gina sat down and gathered her eight Novitiates so she could share something special with them.

"When I was in my fourth year, Reverend Mother Pia was my Mother Superior. She told me then that there was something I needed to know. Something I needed to know about what I was getting myself into. She told me about her experience raising Sister Kitty. You have all heard the name before. Kitty is so beautiful when you meet her in person. I actually had her in my second class for about a year. And, as Mother Pia pointed out, she's *not human*."

No one dared to breathe. They thought, "Well, if she's not human than she must be an …." Their hearts began to pound. They all realized what their Reverend Mother was telling them about Kitty. It was the ultimate display of trust given to them by Reverend Mother Gina. Wordlessly and in unison, all eight Blessed-Sisters circled around Gina and hugged her. They were one.

After dinner that night, Gina dismissed her group by saying, "Go home to your families tonight. You all need to be with them now for their help and guidance. I took the liberty of moving your flights up and notifying your families of your times of arrival so they could make arrangements to come get you. I want you all back in two weeks. If you don't come back, well, you will be deeply missed. If you do come back, please be ready for your assignments! I love you all. You were wonderful student Sisters, easily the best class I've ever had. Thank you all."

The Blessed-Sisters, now a little wiser, showered, packed and left for their homes to reflect on their training and to decide on their individual futures.

* * * *

Two weeks later, all eight Blessed-Sisters had returned eager and willing to embark on a journey as a soldier in His Army. However, each realized rather quickly that Reverend Mother Gina had been crying and looked disturbingly upset. "Thank you all for coming back. Unfortunately, we were called upon to serve in a very serious emergency situation. Please don't unpack; we have to leave at once."

Gina was despondent. She could barely catch her breath. "Sisters, the person I've mentioned over the years, Sister Kitty, was severely beaten and raped repeatedly. She is near death and needs to be guarded at the hospital."

The Sisters could not believe their ears. Gina quickly spoke saying, "This is part of what we do. Sometimes our responsibilities will take us close to evil but we are strong in Him and we've been granted 'Special Powers' to help us carry out our duties. And we're going to need them as this may get dangerous. All of Heaven will be watching."

Newly ordained Sisters Bernie T.C., Fran, Sarah, Dee, Pat, Ann and Gabby grabbed their suitcases and boarded the bus. They were acting strong and with purpose, even if privately they questioned how they would ever be able to hold up to this assignment.

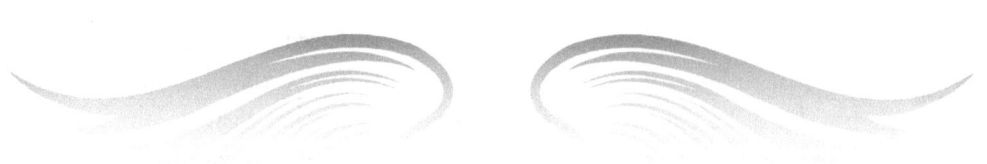

THE ORDEAL

The old man abruptly stopped the service elevator on the top floor. He and his wife knew that the upper three floors of the building were vacant because they were being gutted and redesigned. The project had just begun and would take at least 18 months to complete. They exited the elevator and clumsily wheeled Sister Kitty out and through the door of the condo in the northwest corner of the hallway.

Upon entering, one's eyes were immediately drawn to the view of a particular building which bordered Central Park West. If a building could intimidate those who glanced upon it, this one surely did. The dark, gothic structure shunned the sunlight and hid in the shadows. It had several large pyramidal spires and a small iron fence sitting atop the building's fascia ensconced with gargoyles. The structure was truly a harbinger of evil.

Nodding to the gothic behemoth in silent acquiescence, the old couple pushed the cart over to an empty aged white bathtub at the far end of the room where they unceremoniously dumped the still unconscious Kitty. There was no definitive bathroom as its walls had been gutted during the first stage of the renovation. The tub, which rested its cast iron weight on cloven hooves made of brass, was positioned next to a toilet. The toilet had a raised water box and a hanging pull-cord for flushing. Both toilet and tub were antiques and still in working order.

The old woman searched Kitty's belongings and found $30, an I.D. card and her beige habit. The old woman pocketed the money, put the habit on her head and in broken English said, "Mar-ree," while walking side to side and leaning forward mocking the way old nuns move – the way penguins walk. This time, in Italian, the old woman said, "Penguino, penguino." The old man, who was eating fried chicken on top of the toilet seat, laughed uncontrollably. So much so that he placed the chicken bucket on the floor so he could move his bowels. This caused the old woman to laugh so hard she almost passed out. After finishing his business, she told him to move so he shuffled about six feet into the darkness with his bucket of extra crispy.

After a few minutes, the old man abandoned his post and went back to eating his cold chicken on his toilet table. Instead of washing up, he brushed back his greasy hair with his dirty hands then wiped his hands on his pants – two short rubs.

The woman went back to work undressing a very incoherent Woman of God, meticulously untying each shoe and removing them from her feet. The same procedure was done with Sister's white socks. She then examined each foot, smelling them and extracting any fuzz from between her toes. She lifted Kitty's body from the side to remove her beige jacket and white blouse. After removing her bra, the old woman gave her a full inspection from the waist up. She even placed a bath towel under Sister's body so she wouldn't have her skin come in contact with the cold cast iron porcelain tub.

The old woman clamped a handcuff around Kitty's left wrist and attached the other handcuff to a 10 foot professional grade aluminum chain which was bolted into the wall above the tub. The chain would allow Sister to reach the toilet which was about 6' away. This was how Kitty found herself 30 minutes later when she groggily began to awaken.

Ignoring Kitty's semi-conscious stirrings, the old woman removed Sister's panties and gave her a rectal exam with her middle finger and probed her vagina with her thumb and forefinger. The old woman seemed to approve both areas as 'never having been touched sexually' so she began to shave the pubic hair in Sister's vaginal and anal areas. The old woman then hung up an orange enema bag with a long black hose. She had filled the bag with dish detergent and tap water then fastened it to a bolted hook on the wall above the tub. It was the same hook that Kitty's chain was attached to. The hose was long with an end tube of hard plastic that was round and smooth for comfortable insertion into the rectum. The squeeze clip allowed the soapy water to rush inside of Kitty. Within seconds Sister's stomach began to swell making her draw her legs up in a weak effort to ease the cramps that were becoming more intense as each ounce of liquid poured into her. After the bag emptied, the old woman began to push down on Sister's stomach forcing the liquid to shoot out of her anal opening and onto the floor of the tub. From there it formed a nasty little river which flowed downstream to the drain. A small groan escaped Kitty's lips as her head once again lolled to one side as she sought refuge in a chloroform-induced oblivion.

The tub had been cleaned before the old woman began to bathe Kitty in a bubble bath. It was while she was shampooing Sister's hair that Kitty fully woke up. It didn't seem real to be in a tub being bathed by someone. "Am I ill," asked Kitty who hadn't realized her left hand was cuffed to a chain. Initially she thought she was in an old hospital being attended to by a nurse. For the life of her, Kitty couldn't figure out why this woman was bathing her. As her head began to clear Sister realized that there was a handcuff around one of her wrists. That's when she knew she wasn't dreaming; she was in grave danger. "Please miss, leave me alone. STOP IT! STOP CLEANING ME!" The old woman just smiled and continued, softly saying, 'MAR-REE' with a crooked smile.

Kitty's mind raced as old woman quickly finished bathing her. The stopper was pulled and the water drained out. Instinctively trying to cover herself with her hands, Kitty gaped in disbelief at her shaved genitalia. Jerking her head up and seeing there was now an old man with the old woman, both staring at her naked body from the near corner of the room, pushed her over the edge. Now Kitty started to bellow. "You two had better stop it right now! I'm a nun, a Woman of God. I am not allowed to be touched in this way so just stop!" She stood up to make her point loud and clear but the old man started walking toward her with something in his hand. On the way he plugged it into the wall and continued walking toward her. When he reached the tub he said something with words that Kitty didn't understand. The old man grew angry and held up the bare end of the extension cord. When Kitty didn't respond to his command he touched her with the exposed wires high on her right arm. She was still standing – barefoot – in the wet tub. The ungrounded current made full contact going directly through her body. It only took a second touch on her middle back to cause Sister's mouth to open while her head gyrated in a circle like a jack-in-the-box. Every other part of her body twitched. It was only a 110 volt outlet but it packed a wallop. Sister collapsed into the tub and stayed there not making a sound. The old man actually touched here three more times while she lay prostrate. Each time, Sister's body convulsed and each time, the old woman laughed. Finally, Sister clutched the edge of the tub and half fell, half stumbled out of the deep tub and collapsed onto the cracked tile floor. She didn't have the strength to rise to her feet.

* * * *

At some point Kitty asked the old woman if she could use the toilet. Aware that there would be no privacy Kitty had tried to will away her biological needs but she just couldn't hold it in any longer. The chloroform and the enema had made her need urgent. The old woman told Sister she could use the toilet but she would have to do her business handcuffed. Kitty couldn't argue; she was just too weak.

Kitty had to stretch up and grab hold of the window sill to pull herself up onto the bowl. She accidentally pulled aside one of the black and heavy ad hoc curtains to see a brilliant, sun drenched part of New York City with a noon sun straight up in the sky. Except for that one building in the shadows. Seeing it filled Kitty with incomprehensible dread. As she dropped herself onto the toilet, the old woman abruptly wrenched the curtain closed.

Doing her business under the scrutiny of the old woman, Sister realized she was overmatched. She didn't know what to do. The pain that resonated from the electrical shock was excruciating and the smell of burnt flesh from her arm and back truly frightened her. The old woman uncuffed Sister from the tub, simultaneously grabbing a fistful of Kitty's hair and yanking her off the toilet. Still holding her hair, the old woman slapped Sister on the bottom and dog-walked her to the other side of the room. In an act of complete submission Sister didn't argue or complain, she just followed on all fours.

On the other side of the room large, raw and gray sections of artist canvas hung from the ceiling like drapes. The canvases touched the floor and enclosed something in the middle. The inside of the 10' x 10' enclosure was well lit. "What's inside?" wondered Kitty. She didn't have to wait very long to get an answer to her question. Inside was a leather covered bench with four weighted aluminum posts standing at each corner. It reminded

Sister of a crude hospital setting with loops on the tops and sides of the posts for hanging drips. But that's not what it was for. It wasn't hospital equipment to help the sick, it was a crude device designed to torture the innocent.

The old woman directed Kitty to lie down on the bench. She tied Sister's ankles with leather straps to hooks on the side of the aluminum posts. It looked as if she was about to give birth. A longer leather strap was fastened to her wrists while being wound through the loops on top of the two aluminum posts above her head. The long strap had enough play in it so Sister could wipe her tears with one hand while the other hand pulled away. After the old couple checked all the ties, they walked out of the enclosed area. Kitty was now very alert and the silence terrified her. She began to feel ashamed. "Maybe God is punishing me for the deaths of my three missionary Sisters. I so loved them. I must have been careless for such a tragic event to have happened. I am so sorry. I will humbly accept any punishment as my penance for not being able to defend my...." Even for an angel in disguise, the mere thought of being outside of God's love led her to feelings of hopeless despair. Sister's biggest challenge was about to arrive. "God help me!" she prayed. Then she drifted off to sleep.

Kitty was jolted awake to a crazed looking man probing her vagina with his fingers. Instinctively, she tried to close her legs but could not. Panicked, she tried to explain herself to this new person, "I don't belong here! I work for God! Let me go!" But the man continued his examination not even acknowledging that she was speaking. She said in a louder voice, "Why won't you listen to me!?" The man, at first, just glared at her with his crazy eyes. Then surprisingly he unfastened her feet from the leather straps. Thinking he was miraculously going to let her go, Kitty remained still lest he change his mind. Instead of freeing Kitty, he removed the larger strap from her hands and tied it around her waist. He tugged on the strap which threw her off the bench and onto the floor. He used the strap to roughly drag her back across the room to the bathtub. Upon reaching the tub she was once again handcuffed to the chain which was bolted to the wall.

The crazed man sat on the edge of the tub. With his left hand he reached down and grabbed Kitty by the arm. He pulled her up and over his knees where he began to spank her bottom with his bare hand. He slapped her buttocks over and over and over again. When his hand started to throb he found one of Sister's shoes and continued his assault.

At first the slaps just hurt but after he started using the shoe, the pain became unbearable. Kitty automatically rolled her body away from the pain to where she was facing upwards. Undeterred he continued the beating by hitting the front of her thighs and lower stomach. Finally, it was too much for Sister. She collapsed onto the floor where she spoke in shallow tones:

> "*S'il vous plaît. (Please.)* **S'il vous plaît aucun plus.** *(Please no more.)* **Je suis dé solé pour le probléme de démarrage.** *(I'm sorry for starting trouble.)* **Je promets d'éter obéissant.** *(I promise to be obedient.)*

Kitty would revert to French when under extreme stress. It was the way Sister spoke to Reverend Mother Pia when she was growing up in Paris. She desperately wished her mother would come to help her. Pia *was* there along with Kitty's best friend Antonia. Kitty could not know of their presence as they had been ordered, by God the Father himself, not to intervene.

Sister was sprawled out on the floor completely naked, battered and bruised, groveling at his feet. She clutched the crazed man's leg in an act of total submission and begged him to forgive her. Internally, Kitty was begging God to forgive her. She thought she had been spiritually abandoned. All of heaven wept.

The crazed man was unsympathetic in spite of Sister's unconditional surrender. "The next time you refuse an order and talk back, I'm going to get my wire cutters and cut off a toe, a tit and your clit." He then kicked her aside hitting her stomach with the point of his shoe, knocking the wind out of her.

Kitty just laid there gasping for air as the old woman came in and again knocked her out with chloroform. An unconscious Kitty was placed back on the bench with her hands and feet bound once more by leather straps. The old woman had administered several injections into her buttocks and thighs. The old couple had stolen a nurse's medical bag that contained a dozen ready-to-push syringes. The medication was a painkiller that also fought off infections: procaine/penicillin. They also iced her down to decrease the swelling. She must look absolutely perfect.

When Kitty began to awaken, the old woman was snickering as she inserted a sausage funnel into Kitty's rectum. The old man handed a little cage containing six small rats to the old woman. Juvenile rats are much more adventurous than gerbils, mice or hamsters, especially when inserting them into someone's rectum. Dropping a rat into the funnel, the old couple laughed hysterically as the rodent's tail disappeared into Sister's anus.

Kitty was already defeated. Her will to fight was gone. She knew that God abhorred humans interacting in that fashion with animals. Even though she did not willfully participate, she was sure that her human form had been defiled beyond repair. She believed her sins were so great that it would be impossible to gain salvation. So Kitty cried and cried wishing for her Reverend Mother to appear so she could advise her on how to get back in God's good graces. But no one came. Sister was quite alone, surrounded by evildoers, with no hope of forgiveness.

* * * *

The crazed man returned an hour later with two other men. She could see their silhouettes on the curtains as they arrived. She could hear their malevolent whispers of conspiracy. As the curtain was pulled aside, Sister knew their godless acts would soon commence.

The crazed man scolded the old man and old woman. "You fucking shits – get those goddamn rats out-of-here – you idiots!" The old couple grabbed their cage and left the canvassed area. He then looked down at Kitty and said, "Good, I want you to be wide awake for this."

Kitty's mind was racing, "What are these men going to do to me?" The crazed man called out, "Hey, are you ready?" A voice answered, "Go ahead." As a different man pushed aside the canvas with his digital movie camera, he looked down at Kitty and realized something was very, very wrong. "Hey man, you sure you got the right chick?" But his question only garnered a dirty look. The cameraman was concerned. He felt it was an important question. So he asked it again, "Are you sure? This chick don't look like a pro. I've never seen her before and I've seen just about everyone over the last 14 years. I mean I own the best porn collection in the entire world. I've seen *everyone* and this chick isn't in the business. Besides, she's pretty but – Chinese, she's over 30 and she's pretty beat up. It's going to be a difficult shoot."

The crazed man answered, "Hey asshole, just start filming and shut the fuck up!" He knew that the crazed man was dangerous with a pit bull's strength and temperament which he could usually calm down but today was different. Today the crazed man had a malevolence about him that scared the hell out of the cameraman. He kept quiet and started filming.

The 27 year Old Sister of Kitty, sensed something had changed, so she turned her head and looked toward the camera. It was then that the cameraman knew for sure that this was a bad shoot. He whispered, "Oh my God, I think she's a nun like the ones that taught me in Catholic school." Fearing for his own life he didn't dare speak. He whispered to himself, "God forgive me."

The crazed man began his performance for real. His penis was large in length and girth and, already erect, the head of his penis only peeked out past his foreskin. His partner was a tall black man with a long penis that had a bulbous head.

The crazed man shoved Sister's body so she now lay on her side. After lubricating his shaft with oil he slithered behind her and abruptly entered her anally. Already shaking with terror and revulsion, Kitty could not keep herself from screaming aloud in agony. At the same time, the thin black man rammed himself into her vagina. Her hymen ruptured and Sister Kitty writhed in unbearable pain.

The men moved in simultaneous but opposite motions. They were in sync, allowing one man to thrust forward while the other drew back. In order to survive this indescribable ordeal, Kitty began to mentally disassociate with what was happening to her. Still believing that this was God's retribution for what happened in Africa, she tried with all her might to obediently accept her punishment. Not knowing what else to do, she prayed. For every prayer she uttered, her voice became stronger.

In a moment of clarity, Kitty realized that the crazed man had scripted this shoot to perfection. "Everyone had a part to play, even me," thought Sister. In fact, the only thing incongruous to the moment was the cameraman. Kitty had caught him glancing over with guilty eyes and a shamed demeanor. He was dutifully recording her sexual assault while knowing it was wrong. It wasn't much but Sister took a small amount of solace from his reactions. "Maybe I have a chance for redemption," she reasoned. "Maybe God is just testing me."

After more than an hour, they stopped sexually torturing her but Kitty *still* had not stopped praying aloud. The black man went off to the bathroom. The crazed man slid out from under Sister, wiped his face with a towel and proceeded to scream at Kitty for "ruining the entire scene by not submitting." He walked around to the head of the bench. Leaning over, he said, "Stop saying those fucking prayers and pay attention!" In order to help understand, he pinched her nose until she had to breathe through her mouth. He then grabbed her tongue and pulled it. This forced her mouth to open wider. The crazed man pulled her head by the hair to the edge of the bench. He then began to slowly place his penis into her mouth for an inch then pull it back. Then three inches in and he'd pull it out. He repeated the process over and over until he was able to slide his entire penis down her throat. Kitty's bound arms were flailing. The rest of her body was convulsing. She was turning blue each time he inserted himself into her mouth. Sister was now in a full-blown panic.

"Please, no more!" she begged. "I'll obey." But to no avail. The crazed man was having too much fun watching her nearly pass out each time he would plow his penis deep into her throat. He loved to watch her eyes roll to white. The black man had returned and thought it was hysterical.

Kitty's neck was fully stretched and exposed by having her head bent back over the edge of the bench. The choking inadvertently caused Sister to shake her head which helped him wiggle his penis through the bend in her throat. Getting stuck there completely choked off her airway. The shaking actually helped him get in and out quicker but it was still a cruel and torturous punishment. Then the black man took his turn.

"Hey, ass-wipe, are you getting all this?" The cameraman answered, "Yeah boss, I'm getting it all. It's a great shot. Good set design. Total submission. But don't forget that we still have a couple of hours of work *after* you're finished." The crazed man was taking one last turn, back on the bench, again doing an inverted blow job. "Okay. I'm about to cum in her face. So this will be my last shot, get it all up close. She made me really hot and I'm about to explode. Her mouth is like a soft wet cunt. " His orgasm was loud and large. It never seemed to end.

After thousands of women and men, he conceded, "That was my greatest performance ever." And indeed, after watching the recording, the cameraman thought it would be considered amongst the greatest pornographic scenes ever filmed. They both left the condo to get a much needed drink and to discuss how the next scene would be shot. To this point they had performed almost 2 ½ hours of hardcore porn.

The old couple perked up as the crazed man took his leave with the cameraman. Their first order of business was to get Kitty ready for the next scene. After being injected, salved and iced, Kitty's entire body was partially numb. Exhausted, confused and alone, Sister had mentally detached herself from the present. She knew that if she didn't, she would never survive this ordeal. The old woman prattled on about what a surprise the next scene would be and how much Kitty would enjoy it. Peeking through the curtained window at the building cast in shadows the old woman started speaking in tongues that shot icicles of fear straight through Kitty's heart.

As she began to pray she heard a sound and that sound befuddled her. The patter of little feet was undeniable. As the child was escorted into the closed area, the old man lifted him up and roughly sat him down on a tall bar stool next to Kitty. The little boy looked confused; he couldn't have been more than three or four years old. Shirtless and dirty, the child gazed down at Kitty and, in an innocent moment of tenderness, the boy reached out his grimy little hand and placed it gently on her cheek. The old man was angered by this and took out his electrical cord to which the child immediately reacted. He tried not to cry, already conditioned by these people that he would be severely punished if he did.

Kitty was barely conscious. She tried to stay awake needing to protect this little boy. She whispered, "It's alright. Jesus will walk you home tonight." Through the eyes of the child two of her closest friends were watching over her. The boy's face streamed with tears of joy as she seemed to have regained her spiritual strength. The Lord and His Amazing Grace was always the answer.

Wanting to mentally torture Kitty into thinking that she would have to perform with the boy, the old man was outraged that Kitty did not fall for it. As he dragged the child away by the scruff of his neck, the little boy twisted around and gently waved to Kitty. She knew he would be alright; a true survivor. "Thank you, God. Thank you."

Just then, the crazed man walked in and began speaking to Kitty, "You've done very good so far, let us tie up a few loose ends and we'll be finished." Kitty felt utterly helpless as she looked around for someone, anyone, but no one was there. The thought of her body being so thoroughly defiled was too much for her to bear. "Please, I think I've already done enough." Upon hearing her words, his thin lips twisted into an ugly snarl. Saying not a word, he reached into his duffel bag and, as promised earlier, pulled out a pair of wire cutters.

In a moment of true insanity, he put the wire cutters around the fourth toe of Sister's right foot and asked, "What did you say?" It was a tactic right out of the Gestapo Manifesto. Something inside Kitty clicked and her helplessness turned into rage. In that instant, Kitty decided that now she would fight back. With her index finger she drew an imaginary line in the air saying, "No more!"

As an answer to Kitty's boldness, he slowly began to squeeze the handles together, cutting deeply into the toe and causing as much pain as he could. Surprisingly, Kitty spoke again saying, "You're demonic and should not be allowed to live amongst other human beings," then she began to pray in Latin. With a haunting gaze locked onto the crazed man, her words were strong and fearless.

Kitty's prayers had started to unhinge him. Clumsily, the crazed man moved around the bench toward Kitty's upper torso and placed his cutters around her left nipple. She had deliberately provoked the man so he cut gashes on either side of her nipple. Even in excruciating pain Sister continued to pray and glare.

At the end of his rope, the crazed man slithered alongside Kitty, gliding the handle of the wire cutters up and down her legs. When they reached her upper thigh for the third time, he turned them around and jabbed the pointed end against her genitalia. Staring back at her with glazed eyes and a slackened jaw, he positioned his weapon around her clitoris. Squeezing the cutters, he nearly severed the most sensitive part of a woman's body. It was literally hanging by a sinewy thread. Sister's pain was now so monstrous, she was screaming without making a sound. Finally, and mercifully, Sister passed out but before she did, she knew she had won the moment.

The crazed man began to pack his belongings and spoke to the cameraman. "Now *that* was fun. We have about 120 minutes in the camera. That's plenty. Help me go downstairs with my stuff and I'll go over your instructions." He yelled over to the old woman, "Get the nun cleaned up and drop her off over by the East River. Don't wait until you get to Jersey, it's too dangerous. Dump all the other stuff into the river."

On their way down the elevator, the crazed man repeated his instructions to the cameraman. "Don't forget to edit to perfection. And I want three copies and the master. There is to be no other copies in existence. Understood?" "Yeah", said the cameraman, "You're the boss." The crazed man was pleased.

Kitty passed out and the old couple started to bring her around so *they* could have fun with her when the cameraman walked back in. Seeing the little boy standing next to Kitty he incredulously shouted, "What the fuck? You assholes! Get everything down to the van and let's get the fuck out of here!!" He then looked at Kitty who appeared to be dead which made him say, "Now we're all going to hell."

They broke everything down as fast as they could. They even took the chain hooks, handcuffs and Kitty's belongings. The sex bench, canvas drapes and wire hanging lines were carted off to the large paneled van and placed in the cargo section all the way in the back. Finally, Kitty and the boy were strapped into the back seat with the little boy looking heartbroken because Sister wouldn't wake up. They had already dismantled and moved the camera – ripping out all its connections – and placing the parts into an exterior storage compartment on the underside of the van. Afterwards, the condo was left looking once again like a construction site.

With the old man behind the wheel, the van had been parked on the sidewalk along side of the service entrance. As the cameraman got in he said, "Don't go to the path by the East River. Make a left and drive to the road just before the Henry Hudson Parkway's north entrance."

The cameraman continued, "I want her body and the kid to be found. It won't matter, the nun is already dead and the kid can't talk. The cops will easily be able to find them on the Upper West Side. Everything else – the canvases, the bench and all the other parts we have will be dumped over in Jersey, somewhere in the swamps. Then we will burn the van and run. So please drive slowly. If we get stopped before all that, we're toast. We fucked-up this job but good."

Ten minutes later, Kitty was placed on a bus stop bench with the little boy. After they pulled out onto the highway the cameraman ordered the old man to pull over. He then made an anonymous 9-1-1 call reporting what he saw.

When the police pulled up to the sidewalk bench the little boy was sitting next to Kitty rubbing her cheek. Kitty looked like death and well beyond repair. The cops had come with lights on and sirens screaming. They looked out the windows horrified with what they saw. Both policemen were sickened by this tragic scene. The third openly wept.

Escorted by a detective, the boy was taken to a nearby children's hospital. A search through the Missing Persons database got an almost instant hit on who the missing child was and he was returned to his parents that very night.

Kitty was taken to a nearby ER. Upon her arrival, the nursing staff matched the description of the kidnapped nun to Kitty and immediately called the Blessed-Sisters' Novitiate. A half hour later, the convent's representatives, Gina and Romy, took Kitty to a private hospital located somewhere in Manhattan. They even hired an unmarked EMS truck to transport their angel.

All things must die in order to be born again.

THE HOSPITAL

The southwest corner of the private hospital is a side entrance for doctors, nurses and medical staff. When you walk through that doorway and look to the right you see a narrow hallway about 8 ft. wide by 8 ft. high and 30 ft. long. There is only one door which is at the far end of the hall. This door is the only access to a windowless, private room which is both quiet and secluded. It is a room that can easily be guarded from unwanted visitors.

About halfway down the hall, the eight young Blessed-Sisters lined up in two columns of four facing away from the door. They were standing their post along with a small but serious Reverend Mother Gina who was leading her charges. While they didn't look like Marines, they were a very intimidating, no-nonsense group. All were barefoot as it literally made them feel grounded, allowing energy to pass through their bodies. They felt connected.

Reverend Mother Gina had been preparing these eight young ladies to assist Reverend Mother Pia in France. The trip to their new home and assignments were put on hold while they stood watch over Sister Kitty. It was an honor to do so.

Behind them, the large door that protected the room was closed and inside lay Kitty. Initially, Sister had been kept alive with drips, tubes, bandages and a ventilator. The whirring hum and clicking sound of the ventilator marked the rhythmic up and down movement of Kitty's chest as her lungs were artificially pump with air. But after Gina arrived everything was removed and disconnected.

Outside, rumors swirled throughout the city that a nun had been kidnapped and raped, then dumped on a sidewalk bench somewhere on the Upper West Side. The paparazzi were going crazy trying to find any information that would have led to some intrusive picture of the poor Woman of God.

A man tried to sneak by the Blessed-Sisters but was abruptly stopped. "It was like I walked into a brick wall," he tried to explain to his editor. "And when I tried to take a picture, the flash bounced back and blinded me. I couldn't see for maybe 10 minutes. Then the head person, a Sister Gina, told me I had to leave and I would have sworn it was The Hulk and Superman who shoved me out the door. But no one else was around." The reporter told his boss that he wanted off *this* assignment because he was genuinely afraid for his life.

Word also had spread throughout the religious community that one of God's angels was raped and tortured by a bunch of psychopaths and that she was holding onto life by a thread. All these events angered the true believers. They were outraged at such bold behavior so they began to close ranks in a solidarity not seen since the days of the Maranatha which was a 2,000 year old movement which became a password meaning "Christ is coming soon." It seems that Sister Kitty's many achievements had become the stuff of legend. Most believed she was a Messenger of God or a modern day Apostle.

While many were saddened by this terrible news they were not surprised. Throughout history, Soldiers of God had been unfairly punished and put to death for their beliefs. This too seemed to follow a pattern confirming their beliefs that someone special was in their presence. Their instincts were right. She *was* someone special.

* * * *

The Blessed-Sisters began to stir in their places. They saw, but could hardly believe, the most beautiful nun they had ever seen. Reverend Mother Antonia Spingola had worked all around the world attending to victims of famines, tsunamis and the AIDS epidemic. She was a modern day Mother Teresa with the same dedication and devotion to God and those less fortunate. As she walked toward them she seemed to glow.

Gina bowed her head in total respect but Antonia embraced her and told her that *she* was the one whose work was being noticed by everyone.

Gina wept on Antonia's shoulder. Reverend Mother Antonia then walked between the lines with Reverend Mother Gina and seriously evaluated each pupil. After her evaluations were complete she stated, "I know you were all assigned to the Paris convent starting next month to work with Reverend Mother Pia. However, Reverend Mother is being reassigned and I'm filling in for her. Reverend Mother Pia is off to take her rightful place in Heaven." The Blessed-Sisters were saddened by the news, wiping tears from their eyes. They were looking forward to working with Reverend Mother Pia and knew that now they would never have the chance to meet the great woman. Antonia stated, "Your assignments have not changed, except, you'll be working with me instead. And I need all of you, and your Reverend Mother, in France and I need you now." Tonia asked, "O.K.?" The Blessed-Sisters were ecstatic. They answered with a resounding, "Yes!!!" "Wonderful! I'm leaving tonight. I'll make your travel arrangements when I get there. I look forward to your arrival at the Paris Novitiate on Friday morning. O.K. then, thank you Gina. Now I must attend to my sister, my sister who I will love forever."

Looking into the room, Tonia said aloud, "Oh Kitty, what have they done to you?" She then crept over to her friend's bedside, horrified by the wounds she saw on Kitty's face and body.

The machines that surrounded Kitty had just been disconnected, as per the wishes of Reverend Mother Gina. One of the techs asked Gina to, "Please allow the ventilator to stay connected." He explained that the hospital staff wanted to give Kitty something to help her breathe, just until the church specialist arrives. Gina answered, "Yes, of course it can stay connected. And tell your aides that the love and care they showed Kitty was greatly appreciated. Thank you."

As soon as the technician left the room Gina reached over and unplugged the ventilator.

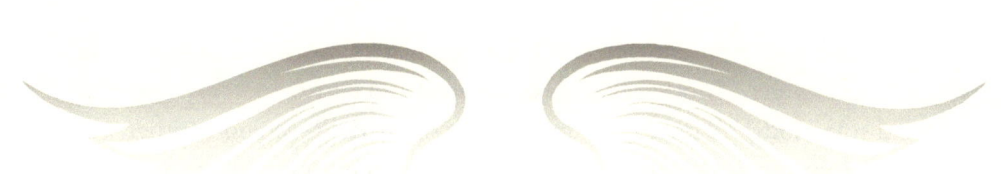

OUT OF NOWHERE

Carmine Spingola was a Mafia Don. He was an intimidating man who ruled southern New Jersey for 25 years. The territory he controlled stretched from Cape May to Philadelphia on the bottom and from Belmar to Trenton in the center. By controlling this gigantic parcel of land his Mafiosi contemporaries nicknamed him Il Duce which is Italian for *The Leader*. Behind his back he was called *Padrone di una campagna* – 'Boss of the farm' – because much of the land area he oversaw was New Jersey's farmlands.

Don Carmine was rarely seen in public. His business was administered with crack efficiency, never leaving any loose ends. The crew he had assembled was fast, stealthy and thorough. They were asked to do their jobs and nothing else. For instance, unlike other Mafia "families," his crew never associated with one another once a job was completed. No one ever knew more than he or she had to know. As a result of his efforts, he was never challenged by local, state or federal governments or agencies. His business ran like a fine-tuned engine. Perfect.

* * * *

Kitty had been missing for five days and, needless to say, John and Sheriff were beside themselves. They had scoured the northeast, searching hospitals trying to find Kitty as they had heard a nun was raped and beaten. No governmental authorities or private agencies had any information on their Kitty. Sheriff had contacted at least 40 surrounding police departments to no avail. Not a peep. It was very discouraging.

John had even contacted the Blessed-Sisters Novitiate in France to update Reverend Mother Pia, his dear friend and Kitty's first foster mother and role model. A message came back saying that Reverend Mother was on her way to America, already aware that something had happened to Kitty. The men were on watch, waiting for some sign or signal that would help them find where Kitty was being kept. But they were preparing for the worst. That night, at about 9:00 p.m., the information they desperately needed finally arrived. It came from the most unusual source they could have ever imagined.

Sheriff was pacing and stomping – literally fighting the air with his fists. John remained seated, frantically trying to hold on when someone began pounding on the front door. Nearly jumping out of his skin at the unexpected sound, John raced to answer, hoping against hope that it was Kitty. Instead, it was Sister Antonia's father, Carmine. Carmine, Sheriff and John were classmates from kindergarten through high school. Old friends who took different paths in life but all wound up staying in Plains.

John said, "Carmine, now's not the time. I'm sure you've already heard that Kitty is missing. We're just waiting for something to break." Hunched over and obviously in great pain Carmine asked, "Do you remember how wonderful you and Carol were to my Tonia? And when my little girl was bullied, how Kitty was always kind and protected her? Please John, let me come in for a few minutes. I have what you've been waiting for – but it's good news *and* bad news. I need you to sit down so you and the Sheriff can decide what to do next. Please John, I have stomach cancer and I'm dying. I've come here only to do right by you." John opened the door to let Carmine in while Sheriff suspiciously eyed his former classmate for who he is and what he does. Looking stricken John said in a husky whisper "Please tell me if she …" Carmine cut him off. "No, no, she's alive but she was badly beaten. I know because Tonia is on her way right now to help her friend. John said he was happy to know Tonia was involved and that Reverend Mother Pia was also on her way. Carmine cut him off again saying, "Oh, Reverend Mother is already there." John clenched his fists saying, "Thank you, Lord."

Carmine told John, "The doctors told me I won't last the week so I had better get my affairs in order. I've lived long enough to see my daughter be filled with the Lord and grow into a beautiful woman. She convinced me to make a *good* confession and she showed me how great God's Forgiveness is. But you have to ask Him for His help."

The Sheriff spoke up, "How are you forgiven for murdering someone? For Christ's fucking sake!" Carmine put his hand up, "Please don't defile the Lord's name! Sheriff, I've never murdered anyone, *ever*. I've never ordered anyone to be murdered. I did order the beating of three different drug dealers who sold to children. But none of them died. And none of those three ever sold drugs again. They have all individually come back to thank me. They said being knocked down was the best thing that ever happened to them. Now all three live clean and simple lives.

"It was easier to let people believe that I *could* commit murder rather than have to explain that I'd never even come close. The things I stole were throwaway items, like surplus wheat. I'd steal it before the growers burned it – which they did so as not to overstock the markets which would deflate prices. I would steal it from them before they burned it, then I'd sell it to foreign countries. The kind of countries with starving children that can't grow their own crops. I was considered a guardian angel in Central America and Cuba. And the farmers I stole from never complained. I saved them from the trouble of burning it themselves, and having to pay for costly disposal permits because of the pollution and the restrictive burning stipulations.

"I never dealt with drugs, street women, loans, alcohol or politics. For a while I did produce and sell porn. And, sometimes, I'd offer protection to people who were being bullied. It's important to know that I never operated outside of my parcel of New Jersey – nowhere else."

The Sheriff relaxed and stepped back. He was shocked by all this new information. Carmine said, "Let me tell you why I'm here. We caught wind of a crazy guy wanting to rape a virgin and put it on film. Like I said, years ago I had a piece of a porn company. We worked with the best porn filmmaker in the world. He was a weasel, but he made the top shelf skin flicks. Thirty to fifty dollars a copy, and he'd film anything. One woman and several men, humans getting it on with snakes, gerbils, dogs, donkeys and just about anything else he could think up. He was sickly creative but it was high quality work and it sold.

"The industry is huge. But one day the guy mentioned filming children so we cut him out immediately. He insisted that the parents of the children were OK with it. And they're not asking for a ton of money. The camera guy didn't get a beating but he was warned that if he was found filming children for smut he would live the rest of life in excruciating pain. Wisely, he stopped.

"Of all the sins I had to confess, my involvement in porn was the hardest to own up to. There is no justification for it and there may be no forgiveness for it either. Its very existence can only be used for improper purposes.

"When we heard porn filming might be involved in Kitty's abduction, we picked him up. He didn't even bother to deny filming some nun being raped but swears he didn't know who she was until the very end. He also said that the guy in charge is absolutely insane. He gave his word that the three copies were the only ones made and the master copy was in his digital camera. The guy cooperated and brought everything, even a beige habit with the name K-I-T-T-Y printed inside."

John and Sheriff were dumbfounded. They hoped there was more, and there was.

"Tonia told me to tell you the address and the time you're supposed to go tomorrow which is 5:00 a.m. Upon arriving, you are to ask for Sister Gina who you already know. Gina will help you. John said, "No wonder they didn't answer at the New York Novitiate, they're protecting Kitty!" Carmine answered, "That's right. She's in good hands. And gentlemen, just one more thing, the camera guy is in my trunk. Do you want him or do you want me to 'take care' of him?" The Sheriff shouted, "No, I'll take it from here." He then helped Carmine get off the chair – got him steady – and gave his old classmate a hug saying, "Thank you old friend."

John and Sheriff helped Carmine get into his white Cadillac where the Don's driver popped open the trunk. The Sheriff grabbed the cameraman and shoved him to the ground. The cameraman hugged the ground, not willing to challenge the Sheriff's noticeable fury.

John shook Carmine's hand, thanking him again and wishing him well with his illness. John was holding the box with the three copies and the digital camera. He also added that he had seen Tonia a couple of years ago and that she was beautiful beyond description. Carmine wiped his tears and drove off into the night. At the same time, the Sheriff dragged the cameraman into John's basement. He ordered him to remove all his clothes. When he finished he was told to, "never speak and just lie on the damp, dank dirt floor until we tell you otherwise, you piece of shit."

Like most old farmhouse basements, the floor was compacted dirt. On the driveway side of the basement stood coal bins. While they hadn't used coal for decades, there were still a few lumps around and a very sticky layer of coal dust throughout the stalls, floor and walls. The Sheriff had found a board which he nailed catty-corner into the horizontal wooden boards of the corner stall. It was actually an old swing seat that he had found on a dusty shelf in another part of the basement. The Sheriff picked the guy up and planted him on the seat. He then tightly tied the cameraman's hands, feet and neck to the wooden slats using some old clothesline.

He looked pitiful sitting on his filthy throne feeling that he deserved every maltreatment and more. He was finished; he had no fight left. He never made a sound and actually passed out from the extreme discomfort. For all his cooperation, Sheriff eventually decided to remove all the cameraman's binds so he didn't accidentally hang himself. He also allowed him to put his clothes back on. In the meantime, John was reviewing the tapes that Carmine had given him, but he had to stop. He just couldn't bear to watch his daughter being violated.

Neither man slept that night but walked into the private hospital promptly at 5:00 a.m. They were greeted by a very vibrant Reverend Mother Gina. "Hello John! Hello Sheriff!" They extended their arms to embrace Gina while thanking her and her Blessed-Sisters for watching over their Kitty. "It was our extreme pleasure to do so. *Everyone* loves Kitty." Gina turned and motioned to her Blessed-Sisters to come forward to greet Kitty's father and uncle. The Blessed-Sisters warmly hugged the men, fully understanding their profound grief. Gina then escorted the men to Kitty's bedside with all the tubes, bells and alarms now removed.

The men were speechless, literally not knowing what to say. Gina asked them to touch Kitty's hand and kiss her cheek. John asked, "Is she dead?" Gina assured them by saying, "Kitty will be fine and would see them both back in Plains on Friday morning. She is no longer in need of medical treatment. We are waiting for a spiritual Healer to arrive. John asked, "Is it Sister Antonia, she's a Healer?" Gina hesitated, "Well, I'm forbidden to speak about that. However, let me ease your thoughts by saying *your* Kitty couldn't be in finer hands."

The men were somewhat relieved. They asked if they could speak with the hospital's Chief Medical Officer. Gina directed them to his office and reminded them, "not to worry."

The hospital official feared this moment. From the time Kitty was brought here six days ago, he dreaded the thought of having to explain to Sister's family the details about what had happened. As the two men walked in with eyes wide and looking for answers, he knew that the time had come.

John introduced himself and the Sheriff to Dr. Robert Wayne, Chief Medical Officer of the hospital. John was very anxious and Sheriff was very angry – ready to pounce. Having seen Kitty bloodied and beaten like an animal had a devastating impact on them. Seeing her lifeless body was too much for them to handle.

Dr. Wayne began by saying, "My staff began to perform standard trauma procedures: a strong antibiotic IV and intubation. We then began to remove objects lodged in her anal cavity but the Mother Superior – Gina – ordered us to cease and desist. She also asked us to leave while she and her 8 student nuns redressed the body with church garments and began to anoint her with Holy Oils and Perfumes." The doctor then feigned a cough to give himself a chance to catch his breath. He continued, "It was sad because all those young girls were working through their tears. But not the Mother Superior. She was stone faced like a warrior. She's quite intimidating."

John spoke up, "What *kinds* of wounds did you find?" The doctor's stomach roiled. This was exactly what he was afraid of yet he took a deep breath and began. "There were five pairs of holes caused by burns but they didn't match the pattern of a stun gun. They were more damaging, like bare wires touching the skin. The depth of the burns indicate that the electricity made full contact. The doctor paused for a moment and it was completely silent in the room. Then Sheriff cursed quite loudly, "You fuckin' son-of-a-bitch," as he stared down the wall. John said, "Please Sheriff, let the doctor talk."

Dr. Wayne reluctantly continued. "The sister was bound by restraints on her ankles and wrists. I'm pretty sure she was forced to wear some sort of collar by the circular scratches and irritation on her neck. Her restraints had to have been very tight. We know this because all four limbs were blue from lack of oxygen when she arrived here by ambulance last Friday.

The doctor was waiting. He saw horror in John's eyes. The Sheriff was pounding the arm of his chair. Dr. Wayne asked if they needed a break but John asked him to, "Please continue." "There were numerous contusions covering most of her body, particularly in the face and abdominal region. She was assaulted sexually by more than one person."

Hearing no objections, the doctor continued, "What I have to say next is extremely disturbing. Are you sure you want me to continue?" John and Sheriff simply nodded. "Apparently, they had metal snips or wire cutters. They cut the fourth toe on her right foot. About 50% of the toe was cut into. They also cut the nipple of her left breast. Like the toe, it was cut about halfway through. Her clitoris was the most severely damaged being cut almost completely off."

With tears streaming down their cheeks, John and Sheriff were done but John had just one more question. "Doctor, *what* was removed from her anal cavity?" The doctor spoke but one word: "Mice." Dr. Wayne turned and quickly left the room. He was an emotional wreck and would ultimately have to take a long leave of absence. The entire time the doctor had been strategically leaving out certain items because he felt it was unfair to her father and uncle. He did not tell them that she had been beaten on the buttocks first with a bare hand and then with a shoe or a paddle for a long period of time. What he had told them were mice were really juvenile rats.

John and Sheriff drove back to New Jersey, anxiously waiting to deal with their *houseguest* in the basement.

* * * *

Note: Reverend Mother Gina knew that Kitty's body was in a dormant state and considered 'sacred.' The hospital staff meant well but her body needed to be: purified, anointed with Holy Oils and dressed in a Healing Gown.

SISTER ANTONIA

Sister Antonia wiped away the tears she was crying for her battered friend. Walking to the left side of the bed, Sister leaned over Kitty, gently lifted her head and began to blow into her face with small whispers of air and progressively larger breaths. These were the initial actions of a *Healer*. The act of blowing is to breathe spiritual life into the severely wounded. Sister continued the healing for several minutes. She even noticed the Blessed-Sisters catching glimpses of the procedure. Antonia had deliberately left the door open hoping for curious responses.

Kitty began to awaken. She smiled seeing her beautiful childhood friend standing over her. In a very weak and raspy voice Kitty said, "Hello my dear friend."

Antonia Spingola had a very awkward childhood. She was tall and lanky with bad skin and crooked teeth. The boys all laughed at her weird appearance and the girls tormented her. Neither the boys nor the girls did anything when Kitty was around. One look from Kitty could turn a classmate into a pillar of salt.

The boys would fare worse. One day after school, a classmate lured Antonia behind some hedges where he promised her a kiss. Antonia was leery but *so* wanted a boyfriend; she had never been kissed before. When they got there a couple of his buddies were waiting. One of the guys had already exposed himself while the others pushed Antonia down to her knees and ordered her to "kiss it". Kitty appeared out of nowhere and pushed the two bullies through the bushes where they both sustained many cuts and scratches. The boy that was exposed was tossed into thorn bushes where the exposed part was – well, exposed.

* * * *

Antonia hugged her friend who she hadn't seen for more than 10 years. No words were exchanged, none were needed. After a while Antonia broke the ice by saying, "You know Kit, there *are* other ways to get attention." Kitty laughed. She didn't realize how much she had missed her friend. "You are the most beautiful human being I've ever seen. Are you really that happy?" Antonia began to cry placing her head on Kitty's shoulder as she had done so many times before. "Yes," she whispered. "And thanks, I was hoping you would notice. You know I've always loved you. You're still my best friend." The two held their embrace for a while until Antonia said, "Look, we've got to do this because we both have places to go." "You have a Special Power!," Kitty was happily surprised. "Yes," said Tonia, "For about a year now."

Sister Antonia quietly prayed. Special Powers were seldom given so she always wanted God on her lips as she used them. She pulled down Kitty's blanket, lowered her gown from the shoulders, and exposed her wounded breast. Touching the lacerated nipple, she closed her eyes and winced with pain. Healers take the pain onto themselves. In order to heal someone they must feel the exact measure of pain that the wounded person endured when the pain was inflicted. And they are honored to do so.

Antonia removed Kitty's slipper and touched the fourth toe on her right foot. Again, Tonia trembled with pain. Kitty noticed how tortured her Antonia had become. "No more Tonia, that's enough. Please my Sister, please." Antonia answered, "So many offered to come and heal your pain. Throughout Heaven and Earth so many humans, angels and creations love you. But no one loves you more than me so I begged them to allow me to take away your pain. You've forgotten how many times you took my suffering away. Please let me do this for you." "Thank you," said Kitty, "But if you need to stop it's O.K. – O.K.?" "Yes and thank you," nodded Antonia. "I'm only sorry we were not allowed to intervene."

Kitty watched Tonia with a quizzical look, "I prayed for you to come and help me. I also prayed for Reverend Mother Pia to come but I just figured that The Lord was punishing me because I shot and killed those two men in Africa. That He wanted me to face my tormentors alone." "We *were* there and we got into big trouble, all three of us," said Tonia.

Kitty couldn't believe what she was hearing. "You *were* there?!," she anxiously asked. "Yeah Kit," said Tonia. "We were hiding in the eyes of the little boy; the poor baby just wanted to go back home. He was sad and frightened and he missed his parents terribly." Kitty cried with joy. "You *were* there – I was so afraid. It makes me feel better to know you were there. But you said '… all *three* of us got into trouble.' It was you, Reverend Mother and …?" Antonia, with a 'gotcha' kind of look said, "Michael." Kitty was shocked. She just stared at her friend waiting for more of an explanation. Antonia tried to explain, "While this was happening all the angels in Heaven grew more and more outraged at those despicable humans. Michael caught wind of what was happening and actually poked his head into the room. The Lord Himself pulled him back with orders not to interfere. And you know how fond The Lord is of His Archangels. Reverend Mother and I felt the rumble and thunder and wound up back in the places we had come from – Reverend Mother to France and me to New Jersey."

Kitty said, "Oh my God!" "Yeah," said Tonia. "It's a little more complicated than that. After your ordeal, all the angels now believe that they finally have their own Magdalene." "No!," said Kitty in a stern and angry voice. "Don't say that, please. Magdalene is so wonderful. I've talked with her so many times before. She's helped me so much …." Antonia spoke up, "Hey Kit, who do you think recommended you for this project?" Kitty was incredulous, "She did? Please don't tease me, not about her." Tonia insisted, "I would never tease about something so important. *And*, I think Michael likes you but that's just an observation that I share with Reverend Mother. That day, the day of your ordeal, he brought his sword and had a look on his face that told us all that this outrage was very personal to him." Kitty and Antonia again hugged both trying to digest all this new information.

Kitty's clitoris had been about 85% severed; it was truly hanging by a thread. The psychopath had deliberately tried to inflict as much pain as possible. After his debauchery, his wire cutters dripped with Kitty's blood. Throughout history, humans have always been creative when it came to inflicting pain on other human beings. Now Antonia was about to literally relive more of Kitty's excruciating ordeal.

Antonia finished up on Kitty's face of swollen lips, cheeks, jaws and throat, the burns from the electrical wires, and attended to her battered and bruised anal opening and buttocks. Now it was time to address Kitty's vaginal area, especially the clitoris which looked angry, wounded and beyond repair. Sister Antonia whispered a prayer for strength as she slid her hand under Kitty's gown. As she reached the area she took a deep breath and began to tremble. She was acting as a conduit drawing the pain from Kitty and transferring it through her body and to her other hand, which was touching her own vaginal area. She was grinding her teeth so as not to let out a scream but the pain was even more than she ever imagined.

All this time, Kitty was regaining her strength. Her concern for Antonia's welfare was also growing. Just like anything learned, a Healer needs time to hone her skills. This healing was a huge undertaking from someone who had recently received her Power. Then, it ended. Kitty jumped out of bed and gently placed Antonia on the visitor's chair where she began to wipe Tonia's face and neck with a cool wet cloth.

Kitty asked, "How was it?" Softly, Antonia answered, "It really hurt, Kit." "Are you O.K. my Sister?" "Yeah," she answered. "But I gotta practice, that was a real test of faith." "You did wonderful my Sister, thank you."

With that, Kitty began to undress Antonia so she could wash her feet, hair and body. Even though it was more symbolic than hygienic, the cleansing was an important part of the ritual of healing. It was a new beginning for the both of them.

THE DEVIL

Ephesians Chapter 6 Verse 2

"Put on all of God's armor so that you will be able to stand safe against all strategies and tricks of Satan."

The Devil exists between moments. The best a human being can do is sense something is awry unless the Demon confronts you directly. Other than that, only the results of his evil deeds are able to be observed. On this day, however, he was especially angry. He hated members of God's Army. So he boldly presented his loathsome self as a clear warning to the younger Blessed-Sisters....

* * * *

The two old friends walked into the shower room arm in arm, literally holding each other up. Kitty removed her hospital gown, then helped Tonia remove the rest of her clothing. It had been a long afternoon and both women were drained from all the activity of the day.

The shower room was large. Nurses used it to bathe groups of non-ambulatory patients. It was complete with hoists and swing seats attached to chains and pulleys. There were aluminum handrails everywhere. Wheelchair bound patients could help themselves get on and off the toilet or make it easy for them to slide into a raised shallow tub. Curtains hung for privacy with long pull rods which made them easy to open and close. The friends entered separate shower stalls and began to cleanse themselves.

Out in the hall, the Blessed-Sisters were becoming anxious. They had stood guard over Sister Kitty for most of the past seven days so, understandably, they too were worn out. However, for the second time this day, the young nuns began to stir. Reverend Mother Elizabeth Pia, the living, breathing, icon of their order had appeared – out of nowhere – right in front of them.

With deep respect, Gina bowed her head but Pia pulled her close and bear-hugged her very successful protégé. She then turned and addressed the Blessed-Sisters, "Hello children." They were completely spent emotionally; it had been an exhausting week. To meet their leader and role model was quite a reward for the hard work they had performed wonderfully over the past four years. This is just what they needed to keep them afloat. "I understand that you're all going to France with Sister Antonia. Thank you," said Reverend Mother Pia.

Reverend Mother was separately hugging each of the eight young ladies, whispering something personal and special to each of them. The Blessed-Sisters were absolutely thrilled. Reverend Mother wanted to make sure that all their families understood that their daughters were going to be in France for a very long time. She told Gina to get them into the washroom so they could tidy up and again leave for their homes for the entire week. Mother Pia also said that she would help Sister Antonia in Paris for a few days so they wouldn't have to report until next Friday. Reverend Mother then announced that Sister Romy Cahill would take charge as the new headmistress of the New York City Novitiate. As always, the newly promoted Mother Superior was standing behind them having already talked with Kitty and Antonia. The Blessed-Sisters were startled by her presence and were now positive that Romy had the Special Power of Bilocation.

After their goodbye hugs with Sister Romy, Mother Pia and Gina led them into the washroom. Out of respect, the Blessed-Sisters lined up off to the side while Tonia and Kitty finished up. Fully washing themselves was the final part of the healing ritual that dated back to the days of John the Baptist. For Kitty it was a very powerful act, a kind of Baptism for a person whose body was unwillingly forced into sinful acts. Tonia also had to go through the ritual because she had taken on the trials of Kitty's human body. But something was wasn't right. Sister Gina was the first to notice two of her Blessed-Sisters were being harassed by someone. In total disbelief, Gina realized it was Lucifer himself. She mistakenly ran at the Beast only to be repelled by his toxic breath which he used like a weapon. Sister Antonia recognized what was happening but was knocked down before she could even take a step. Reverend Mother Pia fell to her knees and began to pray for Divine Intervention knowing the tremendous power of the Beast and the grave and immediate danger to the Blessed-Sisters.

Satan had quietly forced Blessed-Sisters Bernie and T.C. to stand in front of him. T.C. was rooted to the floor. She wanted to scream but was sure her tongue had been cut out and her mouth sewn up. Bernie had also been rendered mute. His glowering red eyes completely controlled the wills of these two young women. He began to humiliate them by mimicking Sister Gina's voice. The Devil spoke, "Look at your new recruits Reverend Mother Gee-NAH." Glaring into Sister Bernie's eyes he repeated Gina's words of admonition, "Be warned my children. The Demon will be especially hurtful around human Servants of God."

Dipping his head down so it rested between the two young Sisters he rasped in a voice so low it could barely be heard, "Compassion, my sweet ones, can only be truly learned by experiencing someone else's pain yourselves. Tonight you will gain true compassion for your beloved Sister Kitty." The two young Sisters were horrified as the Beast forced them to look into his face while he began to molest them. The other six Blessed-Sisters were paralyzed with fear and unable to move an inch while being made to watch his loathsome actions. He promised *they* were going to be the next ones to learn what compassion really is.

There is no way to measure the physical presence of the Devil. He effortlessly held 11 women in place against their will. His actions were slow and deliberate, designed to confound the eye and confuse the mind. Blessed-Sisters T.C. and Bernie were helpless under his immense power and shuddered with revulsion at his touch. Lucifer, delighted at their reaction, slowly raked his talon-like nails over their bodies. His fetid breath burned their cheeks as his hands violently forced their way between the young Sisters' legs. Leaning back so they could see him, the Devil began romancing his victims, smiling at them both in his own distorted impersonation of love. It was crucial that he brought the women to the point where they would question why God abandoned them. His moment of victory would be when they denied their God. Then, and only then, he would greedily take over their mind, their heart, their spirit and ultimately their soul.

The Demon hated God's Army. He called them liars and hypocrites and vowed to prove it over and over again. If you were close enough you could hear him laud his own acts with a chortle and a smirk. In the blink of an eye he could turn violent. Or, he could morph into your mother or best friend just to lure you into trusting him. Make no mistake, he is evil personified.

Being an angel, Kitty completely understood what was happening. She knew that human beings were no match for a supernatural being and she needed to act quickly. She first helped the very disoriented and bruised Tonia and Gina to their feet and had them kneel with Mother Pia in prayer. Then Kitty shouted and clapped toward the six Blessed-Sisters, "Allez! – Allez! – Allez!" which is French for "Go!-Go!-Go!" It was just enough to get the six Blessed-Sisters out of their trances. She ordered them to kneel behind the older Sisters and join them in prayer. Then she turned to face the Monster.

Sister had been trying to knock the Beast off his game, trying to distract him, and it worked. Kitty had turned his focus onto her. With great skill and efficiency, Kitty began to speak in slow measured words saying, "Lucifer, stop. Do not hurt them, they are innocent. Take *me*!" The Beast curtly answered, "We've already had you. During your ordeal, didn't you recognize our handiwork? It was so much fun deflowering our brother Michael's murdering whore."

Kitty knew Lucifer when he was an Archangel and that he was God the Father's first and greatest creation. The name He bestowed upon him, Lucifer, means 'the light'. The Devil always refers to himself in plurals. Here he was making reference to his horde being of one mind. While he was speaking, Kitty managed to get the two traumatized girls to safety. Then she spoke, "I haven't seen your brother for many years. I can't imagine him even remembering my name. But *you* should remember me because when I was no bigger than a cherub you held me in your arms.

You were so wonderful and beautiful then. Lucifer, what happened? How did it ever get so sinfully complicated?"

The Beast was slightly rattled. "Never mind that; that's old news. We're past that now and we've moved on. Your God betrayed us!" "Oh Luci," said Kitty, "God didn't betray you, you betrayed your God. He gave you everything: love, respect and every Special Power, including Free Will. You were nearly as beautiful and as powerful as God Himself! The one exception was that you can never be as great as God, which is of course, impossible. No creation can ever be as great as his Creator. Even angels have boundaries. You couldn't accept that and now you can only exist outside of Paradise, in negative space, reviled as a hideous monster."

The Devil will viciously attack the senses of human beings. He is a shape shifter and chameleon. He can make himself both hideous and beautiful. He is especially skilled at psychological warfare. Satan will mock those you love, while reminding you of things you are ashamed of. He will cut you repeatedly until your emotional wounds flow blood red. Kitty wasn't afraid for herself but she knew her human friends were in great jeopardy. Appearances by the Devil himself were seldom, if any, at all. He is a master of stealth, his only weakness being his pride.

The Beast had finally come unglued. "Fuck you – whore," a very angered Satan shouted at Kitty. "We're greater than your God! So don't worry about us. We're fine with living amongst the heath. We couldn't persuade any angels to come with us because angels are created to be servants and slaves. But humans are so corruptible. It's in their nature to be evil. Your God made a mistake with that Free Will nonsense. We will rule all of humanity one day – soon." Satan was referring to his failure to recruit any angels for his rebellion but found human beings to be easy conquests. Adam and Eve represented all humanity when they submitted to the Devil's temptation. It was the Fall of Man.

The Devil was ready to lash out hissing, spitting and growling. With great conviction, Kitty strategically repositioned herself between Lucifer and the Sisters. As she moved, Kitty tore away her human disguise exposing the head and torso of her angelic form. The Blessed-Sisters were stunned at the beauty, power and splendor of an angel. Kitty majestically rose above the shower room floor and glared down at the Demon. With her right arm raised, Kitty crossed her fingers and curled her thumb announcing God's

Truth and Justice. She allowed her radiant body to cast the shadow of her hand onto the face of Satan, marking the Beast to his extreme displeasure.

Now Kitty spoke in commanding tones.

"Luciferius! Dominus Noster creavit me quo modo creavit te. Ius tibi non esse videris oblitus caelestibus." *("Lucifer! Our Lord created me just as He created you. You seem to have forgotten that you have no power over celestial beings.")* Kitty became louder. No one had ever seen her become so enraged.

"Vestris malis reservatur solum pro entibus cum libero arbitrio. Ego sum Angelus! Nunc abierunt hinc!" *("Your evil is reserved **only** for beings with Free Will. I – am – an – angel! Now – Be gone from here!")*

Kitty had held her ground effectively holding Satan back. Then, another surprise. They flew in from the back end of the shower room in single file. The seven entities encircled the Beast. They looked like flattened owls, circular in shape like dinner plates. They were literally feathered discs with two serious eyes staring out. These beings could also shrink to the size of a golf ball. Around the Beast they flew the way cowboys would circle their wagons. In this case, not to keep the enemy out, but to imprison the enemy within. As the beings came to rest, they became hotter than seven suns. Speaking as one voice they repeated: "Be gone Satan. Be gone Satan. Be gone Satan…." The Beast knew he had lost the battle. As quickly as he came, he was gone. He was expelled by angelic Servants of God, the Seraphim. The Devil changed into a two dimensional entity, a movie screen character but not projected. He just hung in midair. From that he shrunk into a line, not a straight line that can be drawn with a pencil and ruler but a one dimensional scientific line. Melting into a fissure in the tiled floor, he was gone.

Kitty turned to see the three older nuns in a state of shock. The eight Blessed-Sisters were in a full blown panic with Sisters Bernie and T.C. on the floor writhing in pain. Sister called to them saying, "Come here, all of you." Kitty extended her arms clutching them in a powerful, protective grip. They remained like that for a time in total silence.

Afterwards, Kitty broke the ice. "Sisters, let me introduce you. These are Seraphim. They are a different kind of angel than the one you are familiar with. They are God's Creations with the very Special Powers of 'Protection' and 'Recall.' When they're not carrying out God the Father's assignments they are a joy to be around." What Kitty didn't realize was that these weren't just any Seraphim. They were her old friends from Heaven. One of them spoke, "Kitty, do you remember us? We used to sing and fly together in Heaven many years ago." Kitty was dumbfounded. "Oh, but it can't be! Is it really you? Yes! You are! You are my little friends. Oh Lord, thank You!" Kitty and the seven Seraphim had all been created around the same time. They grew-up together in the throes of Paradise, with Kitty being their older sister. The Seraphim began to rub their feathers against Kitty's cheeks which was a high sign of love and affection.

Kitty asked, "But how did you get here?" She'd find her answer in the most fantastic occurrence – which was about to happen. Kitty's outburst would have profound consequences for her future in the way she would serve The Lord. She had finally learned to appropriately use her powers. It was a coming-of-age moment for Sister Kitty.

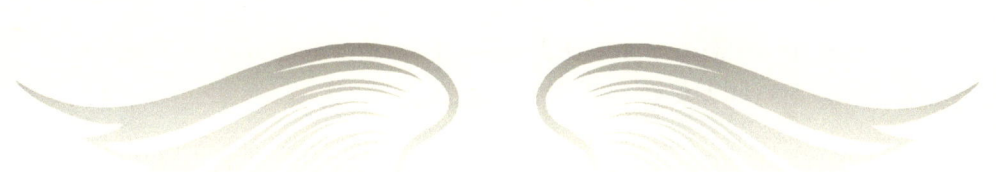

THE ARCHANGEL

The Archangels were God's first creations and Lucifer, the very first to be created. He was knighted with the name Lucifer and he was God's shining light. The Lord granted him all the Special Powers. Most believe he was indeed the only angel known to have been granted Free Will. However, the burden of temptation that comes with Free Will proved to be too great. He chose to challenge his God's greatness and, as a result of that act, he was physically thrown out of Paradise. After that, we only know that The Lord wept. He had lost one of His children to a sinful act.

The other four Archangels remain steadfast and loyal. Just like Athos, Porthos, Aramis and D'Artagnan, the Archangels are aptly named: Gabriel, Uriel, Raphael and Michael. Each has a unique set of responsibilities. Michael's duties included protecting all of God's creations. He is always depicted with a flaming sword, casting his brother, Lucifer, out of Heaven. *"Ego veni propter kaput tuum"* — "I have come for your head."

The face of God the Father cannot be looked upon so it makes sense that God created these wonderful guardians of His Truth and Justice. God the Holy Spirit embraces the feminine spirit. Like air, She forever surrounds us but we can't see Her. She is the spiritual energy on Earth that allows us to live. God the Son, Jesus, is God's human form. As far as we know, Jesus Himself has only needed to come to Earth once since man was created. There is a promise of a Second Coming of Christ at the end of time for the Final Judgement.

Make no mistake about it, in Heaven, Archangels are treated with reverence. They are sent on assignments to different worlds to protect humans, angels and other beings. They are also Heaven's ambassadors who carry The Lord's announcements throughout creation. Archangels are not just beautiful, they are powerful, smart, loyal and magnificent. They are Heaven's Special Forces.

* * * *

The Blessed-Sisters were silently leaning against the near wall of the shower room just inside the entryway. Instinctively lining up in a single file, they were subconsciously giving Mother Pia, Tonia and Kitty the space to draw strength from each other. Reverend Mother so loved her Kitty that her ward's horrible ordeal probably pained her the most. Antonia had proved her love for her friend and Gina was happy just being part of such a wonderful sorority.

The Blessed-Sisters started to feel a very powerful presence within the shower room. They were all understandably frightened and collectively thought, "Lucifer." The older Sisters had also noticed something and anxiously waited to see what was going on. Suddenly the far end of the shower room began to grow dark. This two dimensional curtain of air seemed like an opaque shadow that had no host light source. It was literally a vertical shadow cast from nothing. A few moments later, the Blessed-Sisters could see an incredible blinding light appear behind the darkness. All the Blessed-Sisters shielded their eyes with their hands but didn't dare turn away because they could sense something extraordinarily powerful was also in their presence.

As the bright light slowly dimmed, the dark veil disappeared the way the sun burns away a morning fog. These two actions left a very large and tall person standing quietly at the far end of the shower room. It was Mother Pia who spoke first exclaiming, "Dear Lord, it's Michael!"

The Blessed-Sisters were incredulous that one of God's four remaining Archangels was in their presence. Two of the Blessed-Sisters collapsed and had to be revived by Sister Gina and the other Blessed-Sisters. Michael just stood there knowing he needed to let everyone absorb his presence. Sister Antonia grabbed a towel and covered herself, mortified that Michael would see her nakedness as a sign of disrespect. Being an angel, Kitty always wondered why humans were so ashamed of their bodies. Michael's human appearance didn't distract her like it did the others.

Kitty was the next to speak while she still had her human disguise pulled down to her waist. Kitty had known Michael from when they were angels before humans even existed. They were both created around the same time inside the throes of Paradise. Michael was a speck older and very special but always looked after the little angels, especially during the time of the Great Fall.

Kitty spoke, "Michael, you probably don't remember me …." But Kitty's words trailed off because a voice, a perfectly powerful voice whispered, "Yes, little Kit I *do* remember you." Sister was stunned. "But you were always so busy carrying out God's assignments. How could you ever remember *me*?" Michael answered, "It wasn't hard to remember how helpful you were guiding all the other little angels in Heaven. And the way you mentored your friends here as I'm sure Reverend Mother, Sister Antonia and Sister Gina would happily attest to." Wide-eyed, the three women nodded in agreement.

Michael began to walk toward the three older Sisters and unexpectedly hugged Reverend Mother. Reverend Mother bowed and said, "Great Angel, it's an honor." Michael answered, "Hello Mother. I want you to know, sainthood awaits you. The Lord told me that you'll be coming back with us. He's very, very proud of you." Reverend Mother replied, "Thank you Michael, but I was privileged to have such an amazing life. It was my pleasure to serve Him." The Archangel then looked beyond her and into the eyes of Sister Gina and said, "Oh, and Sister, your work with these young ladies has been acknowledged in Heaven." Gina lowered her head saying, "Thank you Archangel."

Michael could hear the thoughts of the young Sisters. They had so many questions. Again Michael spoke, this time to the Blessed-Sisters directly. "All your questions are perfectly understandable but I'm forbidden to answer most of what you ask except to say that *Judas Iscariot* is back with us in Heaven. All he had to do was ask God for Forgiveness. Our Lord loves when sinners honestly and humbly ask for His Forgiveness and openly welcomes strays as they return to His flock. Man has always underestimated the power of God's Forgiveness. I only wish my older brother, Lucifer, would ask for Forgiveness…." Michael's words tailed off as he wiped a tear from his eye. Angels don't have the ability to cry as humans do, however, Michael was ensconced in human form and therefore, could finally release thousands of years of sadness over his lost brother.

One of the Blessed-Sisters whispered in a strained voice, "Michael, your sword is on fire!" Blessed-Sister Bernie's words startled everyone but she was right; the sword seemed to be burning. Controlled orange flames tightly surrounded the sword. It was a lot like a chemical fire which emits a smell but burns nearly invisibly. Michael turned toward the far end of the shower room to look at the sword. He turned back toward the Blessed-Sisters and said, "That's not fire little ones, that's The Holy Spirit. Children! Behold your God, God the Holy Spirit!"

The Blessed-Sisters froze in their places and were rendered mute. Michael continued, "Everyone thinks I cast Lucifer and his followers out of Heaven but it was the power in the sword that did the deed. The sword holds God's Truth and Justice. The sword is swift to take action defending those beliefs." The Blessed-Sisters were still in a state of astonishment so they silently stood their ground with their heads slightly bowed.

Michael just smiled and looked toward Sister Antonia. "You were described by someone in Heaven as having a glow but to meet you in person is incredible. The once ugly duckling has truly transformed into a beautiful swan. You are a shining example to these young Sisters to how being one with The Lord is so very rewarding. I guess you would have to be special in order to fill the very large shoes of our Reverend Mother Pia. Sister, I'm allowed to tell you that before this day's night ends, your father will be with his Maker in Paradise." Antonia fell to her knees. She wept uncontrollably into her hands knowing that her father had made a good confession, a confession where you're willing to change your sinful ways. Sister had been afraid that her father's questionable lifestyle would keep him outside the Gates to live amongst the heath for all eternity. It was incredibly good news and a wonderful surprise. Kitty helped her friend back to her feet where Antonia whispered to Michael, "Thank you."

Michael asked Antonia to take caution. "Oh, and Sister, please be careful with your Special Powers. It has been said that a multitude of angels defected to Lucifer's rebellion against God. I assure you *no* angels joined his cause. His hoard was literally a cloned army of Lucifers. The power of Bilocation allows an angel to be in more than one place at the same time. The warning label to such power is: If a host entity crosses paths with his clone, than that clone would become subservient to his host. My oldest brother deliberately did this over and over to create a huge following to fight against Heaven. It was his Antichrist Army. His plan of course, didn't work. No creation can trick God but they can break his heart. God the Father wept. It was then that God the Holy Spirit charged me to pick up the sword – the very one you see here glowing – and deliver swift and final justice on those clones and its host. It broke my heart to do so.

"Lucifer had been granted all of God's Special Powers but he abused the honor. Since then, only the Blessed Mother has been granted all Special Powers. Other than those two entities, Special Powers have only been given to a very select few. Bilocation, Rapture and Healing are the three most given to human beings. I can't speak of angelic Special Powers; you wouldn't understand them anyway. However, I can say that neither angels nor humans can have more than any two Special Powers.

The Great Angel continued, "The worst sin a human being can commit is to lead another to their spiritual death. In Heaven, the worst sin an angel can commit is to lead another angel to betray God. The concept of existence without God is pure folly. There is *nothing* without God."

While the Devil strikes fear in the hearts of humans, angels have no need to fear Satan or his brood. When Satan was expelled from Paradise it was more symbolic than as a result of any impending danger. While Lucifer appeared malevolent to the Blessed-Sisters, Michael was glorious, like something out of Greek Mythology. A fierce but intelligent warrior.

Michael looked directly toward the Blessed-Sisters. "Human beings are given a lifetime of choices through Free Will and, as a result, God offers humans Forgiveness. Angels can refuse their placement in Heaven. It's a different kind of Free Will. Limited. Angels are allowed to make a one-time decision called: Self Determination – one chance to choose another *level*. Other than that, I'm not permitted to discuss this matter any further."

Michael grabbed both of Kitty's hands. She could feel his inner power run through her body. "Little Kit, I tried to stop your ordeal but The Lord pulled me back and ordered me not to interfere. The outrageous acts angered me so much that He said I could come back to this world afterward to give you three messages."

Kitty's head was spinning. "The first message," said Michael, "is directly from Our Lord. He asked that when you get back to Heaven, let the other angels fly with you. Let them touch your garments. Instruct them and lead them in song." Kitty was stunned, "I will happily do whatever The Lord wants me to do."

"Secondly," said the Archangel, "Magdalene asked that when you get back – and after you've honored The Lord's wishes – please go and see her. She has a million things to discuss with you." Magdalene, truly heroic during the time of the Crucifixion was Kitty's friend and mentor. The summons by her was an immense honor bestowed upon Kitty and the angelic Sister was thrilled beyond description. The Great Angel had one more arrow in his quiver.

"And thirdly, … well," Michael seemed at a loss for words. "After you've completed those two tasks you still have to come back here to finalize your family affairs and to gain closure for all the time you've spent here. After all that, I want you to come and see me because I want to speak with you about some *things*." Kitty's emotions were bubbling over. She could barely breathe. "Michael, I don't know what to say. I didn't even think you'd remember my name." "Kitty," stated the Great Angel, "It's Kitty and I've thought about you forever." Now the Great Angel wanted to shed his human skins. His inner light was burning through them.

"Kitty, and ladies, I'm sorry but I have to get Reverend Mother back home. Sister Gina, you have to get your Blessed-Sisters moving and Sister Antonia you're leaving for Paris. Now, I seem to have lost seven seraphim and a baby cherub. Can anyone help me?" Kitty said, "I understand Michael. Thank you. And I know where your seraphim are." With that, the seven seraphim flew out from behind Reverend Mother. "Hello Michael, Hello Michael, Hello Michael, Hello Michael, Hello Michael … we were hiding behind Reverend Mother's habit. Hey Michael, Hey Michael, Hey Michael … can we sing just one song please, please, please?" Michael said, "It's O.K. with me if Sister Kitty says it's alright." Kitty took charge and said, "We have just enough time for one song – so how about "*Six Little Ducks?*" "*Six Little Ducks*" was a children's song that Kitty had taught them and it was always a lot of fun to sing. It was a song Kitty and her seraphim friends sang in Heaven many, many years ago. The seraphim were delighted, "*Six Little Ducks*" – yes, yes, yes Kitty, that's the perfect song to sing today!" The seraphim – with the baby cherub in tow – formed a big circle with the Blessed-Sisters, Gina and Antonia. Kitty and Michael conducted the song from the outside and Reverend Mother took her place of honor in the middle.

They started the song with rhythmic handclaps. Then, Kitty and Michael shouted out: "One! Two! Three! Four!" Everyone joined in. The circle became a moving wheel and the wheel became a military guard of honor marching for Reverend Mother. The last verse was whistled just like the soldiers in the movie "The Bridge on the River Kwai." During this beautiful pageantry a transparent stairway to Heaven had appeared in the back of the shower room. Toward the top of the stairs golden rays beckoned for Heaven's newest member. It was a perfect ending to a wonderful reunion of old friends and great fellowship for everyone.

As Reverend Mother walked toward her final reward, Michael, the seraphim and the baby cherub led the way. They looked back at Kitty with waves and smiles. Antonia, Gina and the Blessed-Sisters witnessed the incredible scene before them, breathless at the beauty of Pia's entrance into Heaven.

* * * *

Kitty went about finishing up at the hospital, thanking all who helped in her healing. She also made sure that all her Sisters were on their way to their destinations. Kitty had to go back to New Jersey to be with her father and friends. However, as she stepped out of the hospital, Kitty found herself in Heaven. Unbeknownst to her, it was by Divine Invitation. She had been stripped of all human skin and was in full angelic form, now more radiant than ever. Looking around, she realized that she had never seen this part of Heaven before. It was completely silent yet beautifully serene at the same time. Falling to her knees, Sister began to pray, rejoicing in the Glory of God.

BACK IN HEAVEN

The bright light didn't approach – it was simply there. Kitty was anxious and then a voice spoke but one word, "Kitty." The angel knew it was God, so she kept her head buried in her arms out of reverence. Suddenly the light lifted, gone in the blink of an eye. Now Kitty was confused and she stood to look around. Off in the distance she saw a small woman who was softly beckoning her to come over. Sister immediately began to walk toward the mystical figure standing in a lush garden with the most beautiful flowers and trees Kitty had ever seen.

Just looking at the woman had a strange calming effect on Kitty. Pure and pious, her smile was warm, disarming and genuine. She was, in a word: perfect. Though she'd never seen Her, the Mother of God and Man was unmistakable. Kitty innocently thought, "Gee, she's even more beautiful than my Tonia."

"Hello Sister Kitty. I've wanted to meet you for nearly 2000 years. Your glow is as special as the seraphim say it is. I'm Mary." The Blessed Mother extended her hand but Kitty fell to her knees and began to kiss the feet of her Mother. Mary pulled her up saying, "I'm just one of God's creations like you. Only God must be praised, not his servants."

Overwhelmed by her mistake, Kitty wanted to run and hide but Mary kept her grounded. "Look over your shoulder." Kitty turned and answered, "I see many of God's creations peeking out from behind the clouds. Surely they are as delighted and thrilled to see their Mother as I am." The Blessed Mother said, "I want to show you something about your new station in Heaven." Mary walked a few steps off to the side then instructed Kitty to wave. Sister obediently began to wave and to her surprise quadrillions of angels and creations popped out from behind the clouds cheering and waving back to Kitty. Once again Kitty fell to her knees clutching the waist of the Holy Mother. "No, Mother it can't be! I'm not worthy enough to be granted such an assignment. It must be a mistake!"

Mary replied, "My daughter, God doesn't make mistakes but should you have doubts and fears, talk to your Father." With that, the Blessed Mother walked off nodding back her assurance that, "everything will be fine."

Kitty was left kneeling in the grass confused – wondering how she could ever take on such a lofty position. Just then, her eyes saw a shadow growing on the ground which was being cast from behind her. She could see it was the form of a human. She looked back over her left shoulder but saw none of the creations that had been there only moments ago. Sister started to look over her right shoulder when she saw the shadow on the ground raise its hand. She could see a circle of light pass through the palm of the shadow's right hand. Well aware of who was standing behind her, Kitty kept her head burrowed in her arms awaiting further instruction.

"Kitty – do not be afraid. Lift your eyes and touch my robe. Let me answer your prayers for strength and understanding." Sister dutifully looked upward and stretched out her hand to grasp the robe of Jesus.

"I think you've brought honor to Heaven with your actions on Earth. You've gained the love of your human friends as well as the respect of all the angels in Paradise. Rise now, and be seen as a leader, as one who has claimed victory."

Kitty's light was shining brightly. Her glow beamed into the vastness of Heaven. God the Son joyfully spun His loving daughter around introducing His prized pupil to all of Heaven. And all the creations rejoiced. There were billions times billions of angels of all kinds, shapes and sizes. To Sister's complete delight, those who had mattered most to her, including Reverend Mother Pia, Mother Teresa, the Blessed Mother and Mary Magdalene were there. Magdalene who was Kitty's best and oldest friend was grinning from ear to ear and loudly rejoicing.

Jesus grabbed Kitty's hands and thanked her for her leadership both in Heaven and on Earth. He then said, **"I know you were concerned about your actions in Africa."** Kitty's heart sank. Our Savior made it clear that while all life is precious, under special circumstances, any creation is allowed to defend themselves or others to the death. **"The case in Africa,"** The Lord continued, **"was a perfect example of the special** circumstances of which I speak. Your three dedicated missionary sisters were being beaten and sexually assaulted and you came to their rescue. You gave those men fair warning to 'stop' which was ignored. As a result you had to shoot them. It was an awful experience for anyone to endure. In this case there was no sinful act committed. Go with a clear conscience and an unburdened heart."

Placing His hands on Sister's head, The Lord spoke these words: **"Remittetur tibi peccata tua. Vade en pace."** (*"Your sins are forgiven. Go in peace."*) It was a 'good' confession. Kitty was rapturous.

The Lord continued, **"Your African ordeal adversely affected your thought process. It was good for you to seek forgiveness and clarification. Now, be strong and continue to help others of your kind."** The Lord then smiled, waved to everyone and, in an instant, was gone.

Kitty is the only known angel, since the beginning of Creation, to have received the Sacrament of Penance. Penance is usually a vehicle for those beings with Free Will who seek redemption. Astonished at all that transpired, Kitty knelt and prayed, again awaiting instructions.

KITTY IN THE BASEMENT

Kitty had been praying in Heaven, but when she opened her eyes she found herself walking down the basement stairs back home in Plains. Kitty stepped into the basement virtually unseen by her father, Uncle Sheriff and Tom, their most trusted deputy and longtime friend.

Walking toward the old coal bins she entered the first bin on the left. At the sight of her, a beaten man with a crazed look in his eyes almost toppled over on the old wooden milk crate he had been sitting on. His pants and underpants had been pulled down to his ankles. As Sister got closer she could see that all four extremities were bound to the coal bin's wooden slats with heavy rope. Around his neck was a dog collar and leash which was nailed to a board behind him.

The sunlight that normally leaked into the basement was limited. A single light bulb hanging from a wire dimly illuminated the cellar, six steps below ground level. The enclosed coal bins received no light at all. This lent an eerie quality to the crazed man. Coal soot and perspiration covered him in a greasy coating of filth. He looked like a poor coal miner after a cave-in; someone in alarming discomfort.

Kitty grabbed an old wooden milking stool and sat down right in front of him. The crazed man said, "You had to come here because of your guilt, you know you wanted it. You always wanted to make a fuck film. I know your type: whores. All women are fucking whores." Sister, however, wouldn't engage him in such crude conversation. She simply stood and said, "May God forgive you and have mercy on your soul."

Turning her back on the crazed man she stepped out of the coal bin with her stool and said, "Uncle Sheriff, this is one of the men who raped me." In response, Sheriff dragged him up the six stairs, through the back door and promptly shoved him into the back seat of his patrol car. He was taken away kicking and screaming, never to be heard from again.

Continuing her progress through the basement, Kitty walked into the larger, middle coal bin. She knew that these two old people were *certifiable* and she wouldn't be with them for very long. The old man was not bound but by the way he was seated, Sister knew he was already gone. The old woman greeted Kitty by saying, "Mar-reee." Then she began to get up thinking that Sister was there to rescue her. The old woman even took her shawl and pulled it over her head mocking Sister and the Blessed Mother. Kitty turned her crucifix around so Jesus couldn't see and then reared back and punched the old woman right in the mouth where she unceremoniously flopped back onto her little wooden crate.

Kitty walked out of the middle coal bin and turned Uncle Sheriff's most trusted partner and friend, Tom. Kitty said, "Deputy, these two were also part of my assault. I think the old man is already dead and the old woman appears to need some medical attention."

Lastly, Sister slowly walked into the coal bin on the far right. This bin was in the corner having two outside walls. It made the bin darker and damper than the other two. The cameraman was sitting there in great physical pain and completely broken spiritually. He was sure he was bound for perdition and well beyond any chance of redemption. The man was not bound by rope or chains but imprisoned by the invisible bars of shame and guilt.

Sweating, crying and disheveled, he was quietly whimpering like a punished child. Bloody snot was running down over his lips and chin while several gashes above his eyes had stopped bleeding but were deep and in need of stitches.

Kitty sat down on a crate and wriggled it as close to him as possible, like a priest about to hear confession. The cameraman recoiled as Sister got closer. He whispered, "Are you the Blessed Mother?" With her eyes wide open she began to speak forcefully leaving no doubt about her true identity. "No, the Blessed Mother is a human being just like you. I'm an angel from heaven, here on assignment from God. All of God's creations are tested in one way or another and this was *my* Test of Faith.

"Tell me, why do you sit here wounded and crying? Even if you didn't know I was a Servant of God, you should have stopped it anyway. Why didn't you run and get help? Why didn't you stop them?" The cameraman began his explanation, "I really didn't know the whole time, but about halfway through I realized you were a Sister of God or the Blessed Mother. I did try to stop them but they threatened to torture and kill me if I didn't shut my mouth. So I continued to film but after that crazy guy left I persuaded the old people to leave you on the Upper West Side instead of someplace where you would never have been found. They agreed but insisted the child had to be left with you. All those people are warped. Really scary sick."

"STOP!" Kitty shouted. "You knew from the beginning that I was being forced to participate. Rape is easy to recognize for a world renowned adult film cameraman such as yourself." Sister slowly rose to her feet glaring down at the cameraman. "If you are truly sorry for your sins you must confess them all. If you want to unburden your heart, you have to take control of your life. Crying, whimpering and feeling sorry for yourself is not the way to bring peace into your life. IF YOU WANT GOD'S FORGIVENESS YOU MUST HAVE A PLAN OF ACTION! Start with, Dear Lord, forgive me for I have sinned."

The cameraman dropped to his knees and rolled around the soot covered basement floor in emotional agony. He was left prostrate, speaking in a strangled voice, "I can't, I can't, God will never forgive me. I'll never get into Heaven. I'm beyond redemption. I'll never see *them* again!"

Sister wouldn't let up. She sensed he was ready to make things right. "You couldn't be more wrong. God loves sinners who are truly sorry. He joyfully welcomes them back to His flock." From the floor, the cameraman looked up and Kitty's heart began to pound. She sensed a major breakthrough was coming. Sister was thinking, "I know what God wants me to do now." She was thinking that the Lord wanted her to be a shepherd, one that lights the pathway to redemption.

Sister asked, "What's your name?" "Arthur," he answered. Kitty looked into Arthur's face forcing him to make eye contact. She asked Arthur, "Did you try to change anything in your ways, your lifestyle?" "Yes," he answered. "After I got home that night, I immediately edited the master copy in my digital camera and made three copies. I had decided it was the last time I would ever work in porn. Completing the order of an edited master and three copies was my final act.

"When I was done, I ran outside and dragged an old 55 gallon barrel to a spot underneath the rear window of my 2nd floor apartment. The landlord uses it to capture rainwater for his tomato plants in the little garden he keeps on the property. I went into my workroom, opened the window and began to pitch everything into the 55 gallon drum. All my porn, the entire collection, had to be burned. I had one of the largest collections in the world. Then, one by one, I threw in every piece of recording equipment I owned. All of it.

"I destroyed it all. It was probably worth upwards of half a million dollars. After I burned everything it felt so good that I decided to burn my digital camera with the edited master and the three copies, then drop out of sight. Before I could finish some guys who work for Carmine Spingola busted in, beat the hell out of me, and threw me into the trunk of their car. They took me to his office where I told him everything about the bad shoot and the noon meeting the next day with the other four people involved.

"The Mafia guys knew me; they knew right where to find me. I worked with them for years throughout the early '90s. The Jersey Mafia got out of the porn business around '95 because the Don had a daughter who was going to be a nun. Anyway, yesterday afternoon I walked into the arranged meeting place which was an old restaurant with a backroom in Newark. Only four of us were there, the black guy never showed. We were supposed to pat each other on the back and watch "the greatest porn video ever made." Then eight of Spingola's soldiers crashed the party and brought us here. I overheard one of them say the cops caught the black dude and handed him over to NYPD for several outstanding warrants, including one for rape.

"I've obviously given up porn forever and want everything in my life simplified. I only hope that God will put me in a cooler part of Hell." The cameraman recited *Proverbs 5:22*. And The Lord said, "The wicked man is doomed by his own sins; they are ropes that catch and hold him. He shall die because he will not listen to the truth; he has let himself be led away into incredible folly."

Kitty admonished the cameraman, "God doesn't need anyone's help to do what's right and just: He is The Truth. The most important thing you can do is to make a good confession. Don't presume that just because you thought about forgiveness everything is fine. Act on it! Fall on your sword.

Give it all up to God. Neither condemn your soul to Hell nor commend it to Heaven. I'll tell you something that you need to understand; God loves repentant sinners. Find the 'Prodigal Son' in your Bible. Then do good works and point other strays back to the fold. Arthur, there's something you're still not telling me."

While Arthur tried to compose himself, Sister began to heal some of his wounds. She touched his nose to repair the break which took away the pain and made it stop bleeding. She also rubbed something into the gashes around his eyes. It may have been mud or soot but whatever it was all three of his deep cuts were healed.

Arthur began, "About 34 years ago, when we were first starting out, I married my love – my one and only high school sweetheart. We were both 18, young and stupid and very happy. I drove a beer and soda truck back then, all around North Jersey. Babs was a legal secretary and worked for a lawyer in West Paterson. His type of practice was realty and Babs was his 'right-hand-gal.' At the time we lived on Mill Street in Paterson. For years Mill Street had been a staple region for the embroidery industry claiming some of the finest manufacturers and fabric houses in the entire northeast. Its heyday, however, was back at the beginning of the 20th century. The industry had endured The Great Depression and both World Wars. By the mid-sixties, most of the shops were either closed or moved someplace where the rent was cheaper. Now, for all of its past splendor, Paterson has a lot of empty buildings, some of which were converted into office space or co-ops with large cattle car style elevators that still work. The city's claim to fame is a statue of Paterson's favorite son 'Lou Costello' located in a tiny park that was dedicated to him for all the help he gave to the city throughout his life.

"We both worked hard. And I can clearly remember impatiently waiting to get back home after work so I could hold my wife and stare into her beautiful face. It was peaceful times for us. Then, just after our first wedding anniversary, Barbara became pregnant with our first and only child. We were really in a state of shock. We had resolved ourselves to the fact that we weren't meant to have kids.

"Our doctor warned us that there could be complications with the pregnancy. There was a problem with 'collapsing fallopian tubes.' He said, 'There would be no shame in aborting the fetus because of potentially dangerous medical ramifications to the mother and serious birth defects for the child. As time went by we couldn't make a decision. We were afraid to research all the medical data available or get other professional opinions. I think we both quietly wanted a kid but weren't willing to deal with all the sacrifices and responsibilities that go with raising a child, especially one with special needs.

"One day we realized that the decision we wouldn't make was now going to dictate the course our lives would take. It was too late. We were at the end of her second trimester and there was no turning back. Our baby was on the way.

"One week later Barbara's OBGYN told us that the child would have Down syndrome and possibly other complications and physical deformities. The time during her last month of pregnancy, we felt terrible. We questioned our decision and admitted we had no one else to blame but ourselves."

"Emmi, named after Bab's mother, was born on December 22, 1972. It seemed like Emmi never unfolded in the womb.

"Barbara's friend Jill was a sophomore at William Paterson College. Majoring in Special Education, she had to take a class called Abnormal Psychology. She lent us the class textbook which was called Psychopathology: A Study of the Diseased Mind. In that class was a discussion group that talked about a couple who wrote a book about their autistic son. In the book they blamed the child's condition on their inability to make a decision of giving birth or aborting the fetus. Their opinion was that the fetus seemed to recognize from the womb through DNA that *he wasn't wanted*.

"Jill said the class even wrote a letter to the couple for more comments but only received a perfunctory two line reply."

Arthur continued, "It was so hard raising Emmi. She was such a beautiful spirit but the Down syndrome and other problems held her back. Babs gave Emmi her entire life. She quit her job and made herself available to Emmi 24/7.

"Our daughter was smart. Unfortunately she was bright enough to know she didn't fit in. She was even shunned by other Down children in her special needs class. We did the best we could; she knew she was loved at home and was close with many of our extended family, friends and neighbors.

"The ultimate disaster occurred two days after Emmi's 14th birthday when Barbara died of a brain aneurysm. My beautiful Babs was gone. My only feeling was, 'God help me – I don't know what to do without her.'

"The special needs chancellor was very helpful. He got Emmi into an assisted living group home where she lived 5 ½ days a week learning how to take care of her own needs. The state paid for half the costs which made it doable. I would pick her up at noon on Saturday and return her on Sunday evening. In the four years she lived there we never missed a weekend together. One day in particular, we got snowed in and spent all day Sunday building igloos and snowmen while plotting strategies for snowball fights with the neighborhood kids.

"My neighbor Josey was a big help with lady things like menstruation. Then, just one day shy of her 18th birthday, my daughter got her *second* wish. She passed away quietly in her sleep as she had prayed to God to take her back to the place where *everyone* fits in."

Kitty gave Arthur a wry look, "Isn't there something else? Something you left out of that beautiful story?" "Yes," he answered, "but I'm ashamed to tell you." Kitty got boisterous, "Why would you be ashamed to tell me. I'm merely one of God's servants. And, *God already knows*!" Again the cameraman tried to get his lower lip to stop quivering. "Just weeks before what would be Emmi's last birthday she said, 'Daddy, no one will love me.' To which I quickly answered, 'Please, silly girl, everyone loves you.' But she continued, 'No daddy, no boys will love me *special*. The boys all say I'm too nugly.' Then she put her head on my shoulder and started to sob. And it wasn't just a cry. It was a deep, painful cry. She was very aware of her social status. For me it was unbearable because there was nothing I could do to help her. Being the protective father, I blurted out: 'If those stupid boys don't know enough to ask you to be their special girl, then I'll *tell* them to do it! And that made her stop crying and become so happy that she actually glowed in wonder.

"Josey suggested a surprise blind date, maybe with one of her classmates. It could be at Emmi's favorite restaurant, Peking Moon. It's a place that has romantic music and a dance floor. So, on the Saturday before her 18th birthday, I wanted to make my daughter feel accepted. I made it to the school, fully intending to have a 'word' with a few of the boys. I needed one of them to give me a glimmer of hope and then I could convince him to make my Emmi his special girl. But I sat in the car, realizing that if I was successful, I would lose the most precious thing – hell, the *only* beautiful thing that I had in my crappy little life. I must've sat there arguing with myself to just go inside the school and get it over with for hours. As the sun was setting, I turned the key in the ignition and headed home.

A week later, Emmi was gone. "She died in the way she had prayed she would. It was quiet and in her sleep. The house matron who found her said she had a peaceful expression on her face. I remember, while returning her to her group home for the last time, she said, 'Goodbye Daddy,' like she knew she was leaving me forever.

"We had a wake which was only one day and held in the living room of her group home. Emmi's three female friends and roommates were saddened by the loss of their friend. I gave each of them little mementos: rings, gold chains and bracelets that had belonged to Emmi. They were thrilled to get them. Emmi's four male housemates were there looking very frightened – so I shot them my death stare. These were the wise-guys that had told Emmi she was too nugly. But one of the guys, Ryan, came over to me and said, 'I didn't think Emmi was nugly, I thought she was beautiful.' He said that the real reason he didn't want to be with Emmi was because he was afraid. 'Emmi was like a *grown-up* and I really didn't know what to do.' The amount of guilt I felt at that moment nearly killed me. I had denied my little girl what she had wanted most in this world and there he was, standing right in front of me. If I had gone into the school that day instead of being the completely and utterly selfish prick that I am, Emmi would have been Ryan's special girl. How do you live with that? How do you ever forgive yourself?

"I had just turned 38 but felt like 138. My bank account was on E and everyone I loved was gone. Broke and alone it was a free fall to rock bottom for me. That's when I was approached by someone in the industry to shoot blue movies. I couldn't fall any lower so I agreed.

"I had always loved still photography and film; it was my favorite hobby. In the early '90s the porn industry had become technologically modern and quite private. The women were now on DVD and they were beautiful. Porn was bought and viewed in the privacy of a person's home. No more trench coats and dark, sticky theaters, everything was near virtual reality. The only thing left was to shoot in 3D which they are working on as we speak.

"In the early '90s, the Mafia made a fortune from porn. They heard the kind of shoot it was – with a real hardcore style - and recognized it as my signature work. Of course, they knew where to find me. I've lived in the same apartment in Newark since Emmi's passing.

"Sister, the world of porn is two dimensional and very addictive. I felt so ashamed of myself that I literally tried to be a shadow in a three dimensional world. And now I'm here, broken and disgraced. That's the whole story except to say I'm so very sorry. I should have tried harder to stop them, especially those two old psychos. Anyway, I'm sorry."

Sister sat up and said, "Arthur, I accept your apology. I think you are truly sorry and you have begun to change your evil ways. You may not know it yet but you have also mapped out a clear and simple path toward your salvation.

"You said that the guys who picked you up took your digital camera with the edited master and three HD copies." Arthur replied, "Yeah, I'll never get them back now." Kitty said, "But your camera and three copies are resting at your feet." Arthur couldn't believe it. Kitty again spoke, "Arthur, you've burned your vast film collection – now, *close the circle*! Destroy those last four articles. They are the final link to your sinful ways. Destroy them by fire and make your confession. God is Forgiveness, that's what His Crucifixion was for. Forgiveness for *you*!

Kitty then extended her hand. She was filled with essence of the Holy Spirit and innocence. He reached out to touch her hand even though he knew he wasn't worthy. Upon first touch, Arthur finally knew this was really happening to him, a sinner on borrowed time. Nothing human was moving, even the sunlight froze in the moment. It was an impenetrable safe haven. Maybe even a slice of Heaven? Maybe even a chance for redemption?

Arthur burned the last of his evil remnants in a 55 gallon drum in the yard just outside the basement. Kitty was gone and a cabbie beckoned Arthur to get into his taxi. As he reached the cab, the driver said, "Don't worry, your fare has already been paid." As Arthur got inside, he noticed two other passengers were in the back seat and he began to cry. It was Barbara and Emmi – and they were crying too. Kitty was there in full angelic regalia. Sister's frosted white hair framed her beautiful face. It was truly the face of an angel. Kitty was invisible to the reunited family. She was crying too.

* * * *

Kitty's time on Earth was growing short. She only had several minutes to say goodbye to everyone she loved. "Daddy, I have to take my leave. I love you so much. I'm happy for you and Mae and the new baby to come. Oh, and by the way, he thinks his name is Sheriff!" With a loving smile John said, "Kit you always leave us shaking our heads. I love you." Kitty hugged him and turned to Uncle Sheriff and Aunt Marie and said, "Oh, and you guys…" Before she could finish her sentence, her father resignedly mumbled, "Oh, no." Kitty continued, "Baby Sheriff will have a playmate when you give birth to your baby daughter." Sheriff and Marie were beside themselves. They had been unable to conceive so the news was incredible! She hugged them once more and said, "Bye for now," leaving a very happy and astonished group behind to enjoy their future blessings.

* * * *

Kitty completed all of the tasks the Lord had given her with incredible efficiency making all the angels and creations in heaven take notice. The time she spent with Magdalene was enlightening. She gave Sister a treasure trove of suggestions and approaches in the way she accepted each new challenge. Kitty also rekindled a special relationship with the Archangel Michael, a matter that was kept quite private.

One day, unexpectedly, a messenger delivered a request from the Lord which sent Kitty back to that quiet part of Heaven. Magdalene advised her friend to, "Stay strong in Him and pray until you receive new instructions. God the Father needs someone special to go back there on assignment." Sister asked, "Mary, I'll do whatever God wants me to do but have human beings lost their belief in God? Have they already forgotten all about God's Amazing Grace?" Magdalene answered, "The only thing I'm sure of is that God will never give up on human beings. They are his children – always."

Placing a kiss upon Kitty's bowed head, Magdalene whispered, "Now, vade ad Diem (go with God)."

A moment later, a kneeling Kitty opened her eyes to find the Blessed Mother standing over her. Helping Sister to her feet the Blessed Virgin said, "The Catholic Church is in a state of disgrace. Our Lord needs you to go back to Earth and this time Magdalene is going with you."

www.ingramcontent.com/pod-product-compliance
Lightning Source LLC
LaVergne TN
LVHW041609070526
838199LV00052B/3054